Worse Than Dying

By Brett Van Valkenburg

brettvwrites@gmail.com
www.brettvanvalkenburg.com

"A hungry man is not a free man."

-Adlai E. Stevenson

I

The violence began like a storm in springtime—a drip here, a drop there, and then suddenly a torrential downpour. And hell for anyone who happened to get caught in it. Within a week, everyone in Barrel County was either holed-up or dead—to some degree. Most of the Barnes family belonged to the former category, barricaded inside their home on the outskirts of a small town in upstate New York.

"I'm going to do a sweep. Will you come?" Noah Barnes asked his father.

Charlie didn't answer. He sat in a beat-up leather recliner staring at their blank TV, his fingertips raking back and forth over the cracks in the armrests. His hair seemed twice as gray as it did only a month ago, and his beard had exploded.

Noah sighed and walked into the kitchen.

His father hadn't ventured outside in over a week—not since one of those things had surprised Charlie from the shadows of their toolshed. His heart nearly stopped when she came staggering towards him, a stick jabbed in her left eye, blood-caked hands groping for food.

Charlie had been handling the outbreak with relative poise until that moment, but the sight of her mutilated, yet familiar face pushed him over the edge. He shut down—stood there waiting for her necrotic fingers to pull the meat from his bones. It was as if he were willingly offering himself as a sacrifice. And maybe he was.

As she grasped Charlie's shirt collar and opened her mouth wide, Noah appeared from around the corner of the house. He rushed up behind the woman and brought his machete down on the back of her head, killing her a second time. She slumped against Charlie's shoulder before falling face-first onto the grass.

Charlie stood there, pale and near-catatonic, his breath entering his lungs in short, rapid gasps.

They'd seen dozens of these things by now—of every demographic and degree of disfigurement. What about this woman had has father so shaken up? Noah wondered.

He took Charlie by the shoulders and shook him. "Dad. Dad!"

As he tried to rouse him from his trance, the woman's dress caught Noah's eye. The floral print looked familiar, like something he'd seen in a photograph a long time ago.

Noah knelt next to the body. Twigs and leaves stuck in her brown hair. A medial laceration tunneled beneath the blood-soaked cuff of her white cardigan. And there was a similar cut on the other wrist. Noah slipped his hands beneath her torso. He was about to turn her over to see what had Charlie so spooked, but he pulled his hands away. He already knew.

Neither Charlie nor Noah had spoken of it since. In fact, Charlie didn't speak again for days, and even then, it was only to mutter a word or two. The sparse communications coming out of his mouth seemed to correlate with food going in, as his already-thin body diminished to a near wireframe.

"Can I go with you?" asked Noah's little sister, Abigail.

"Sorry, darling, but it's too dangerous," he said as he looped a machete sheath around his belt.

"But how come you get to go and I don't?"

"Because I have to. Believe me, if I could stay in here with you, I would." Noah looked at his father out of the corner of his eye and said, "but someone has to keep us safe." The subtle dig elicited zero reaction from Charlie.

Abigail's face soured. "Hmph.".

"Don't pout, Abby," he said patting her curly brown hair. "If everything's quiet, I'll take you out for a walk after lunch."

"Fine," she drawled and then clomped away.

His brow furrowed. I'll take you out for a walk, he thought. It was bad enough he hadn't the patience to carry on with her bootleg homeschooling after their mother died, but now he was starting to regard her well-being as if she were an old dog he'd grown tired of. There was just too much to do around the house. It wasn't fair—to anyone.

A Regal 700 rifle leaned against the refrigerator. Noah picked it up and slung it over his shoulder. He rarely used the gun, but he always carried it with him just in case.

Some people might have thought that Noah's family was lucky. His father spent over twenty years working for the local firearm manufacturer, Regal Arms, which gave him access to steep discounts on all kinds of long guns. A pathological bargain-hunter, Charlie unconsciously became a gun collector simply because the deals were too good to pass up. His collection became so bloated that he had to hide some of his more extravagant purchases from Barbara. One such covert, prized purchase was Charlie's bulky Regal Sedona rifle.

"What's this gun for?" Noah had asked Charlie, examining a four-inch tracer round that fit the gun's caliber. It was the largest cartridge he'd ever seen.

Charlie inserted a swab into the rifle's bore. "Big game—elk or bear."

"Seen any elk around here lately?"

His father smiled. "Not lately."

"Then why buy it?"

Charlie paused. "Why not?"

"And what did mom say about it?"

Charlie leaned in close and, in a hushed tone, said, "What your mother doesn't know won't hurt me."

Noah chuckled. He had put a finger to his lips and winked.

But anyone who assumed that a massive stockpile of munitions was vastly advantageous would have been wrong. At the beginning of the end, the Barneses had only fired a few rounds before figuring out that the undying were attracted to sound. Shoot one and an hour later three more showed up to investigate the noise. A single bullet wasn't worth the temporary safety or immediate convenience. Once Charlie and Noah discovered this pattern, they began dispatching each corpse with a blunt blow to the head. Afterward, they burned the bodies in a clearing on their property, far back from the road.

What was advantageous was the house's semi-rural location, nestled on a hilltop that offered a vantage overlooking the highway. Shortly after graduating high school in 1975, Charles Barnes and his wife, Barbara, reluctantly purchased a seventy-five-year-old fixer-upper just a few miles outside the town of Lyons. While starting a family in such an ancient house wasn't their first choice—wasn't even in their top five—it was all they could afford on Charlie's assembly lineman salary.

But four decades later, the property's inconvenient location turned out to be an asset when people began dying—and then undying. The Barnes family still encountered their share of living dead, but in numbers far fewer than the people holed-up in Lyons proper.

Noah squinted through a crack in the wood slats covering the window on their front door. No movement. He stepped outside and quietly closed the door behind him.

Noah never knew what to expect when he left the house. Most of the time it was safe, but sometimes they would be lurking—usually near the old doghouse. A chained dog was an easy meal. Whether that was something they learned or knowledge retained from life, Noah could only speculate.

Sometimes there would be two or three. Whenever that happened, Noah darted up the hill adjacent to the house. The trespassers invariably gave chase, but the hill was steep enough to trip them up, making them easier to deal with from the high ground. Any more than three and the Barneses would sit quietly until they moved on, which sometimes took all day, and that wasn't easy for a seven-year-old.

Noah circled around the house before moving into the front yard. With no sign of immediate danger, he headed down the driveway. Noah turned up a wooded path running alongside a creek that flowed from the direction of the burning grove, where the dead would occasionally enter the Barnes' property through the woods and then linger near any smoldering remains.

Through the forest canopy, Noah spotted a few turkey

vultures circling beneath the cloudy sky. Up ahead, a coyote darted across the path followed by a pair of rabbits. A moment later, three doe jumped over the brush on the other side of the creek. They hopped through the water and bolted right past Noah, ignoring him completely.

He rubbed the umber stubble on his chin. It's like they're running from a forest fire, he thought, and then he stopped hard in his tracks.

Noah looked in the direction the deer had come from. Flashes of red fabric appeared through the undergrowth. He hid behind an oak tree and waited for it to come nearer. It moved too fast to be deceased, even if only recently, but that didn't make it any less threatening.

Suddenly, a balding man with a sandy beard came flailing through the brambles. His buffalo plaid shirt was tattered and covered with burdocks. He stumbled into the creek-bed, cutting his knee on a rock.

"Motherf—!" He yelled in anguish.

The heavyset man labored to his feet, took another step, and fell again. He cried out in pain once more before finally getting up, plodding through the water, and collapsing on the opposite embankment.

As he watched the man splayed out on the dirt gasping for breath, Noah knew what was coming next. The dead were on baldy's trail, but how many? In the near distance, leaves rustled and branches snapped.

If there are more than two, he thought, I'll have to let them have him.

One after another, three corpses came staggering out of the brush. Noah pursed his lips and issued an inaudible damn it. They were his neighbors, the Fitzpatricks, from down the road. They stumbled down the bank and into the creek.

Mr. Fitzpatrick was missing a large chunk of flesh from his neck. His head lolled toward the opposite side of the marbled bite-wound. Mrs. Fitzpatrick's nose had been bitten off, leaving a hood of reddish bone over two narrow, black slits. Bloody holes in her blouse led to mouth-sized pockets in the flesh beneath. Their teenage son Hunter, in addition to various bite wounds, had his forearm torn off. Tattered skin and tendons hung from the boy's humerus like party streamers. As bad as they looked, he'd seen worse.

Predators and prey were completely engrossed in one

another, and Noah knew he could easily slip away unnoticed. He hadn't crept more than a few paces downstream when the chubby man began blubbering. Noah stopped. He closed his eyes and exhaled deeply before turning back to the hunt.

As the trio slogged through the creek, Noah switched off the rifle's safety, took aim at Mrs. Fitzpatrick, and fired. The bullet went clean through her skull. Her body splashed into the shallow water, falling against a bed of rocks. Unfazed by the demise of their matriarch, father and son Fitzpatrick remained wholly focused on their impending meal. The camaraderie of the dead, it seemed, was exclusive to the animate.

He fired again and missed. The receiver spit out a used shell as he slid the bolt back and forth. The last bullet pierced the father's side, but Noah knew that wouldn't be enough. He dropped his rifle and sprinted toward the creek.

Mr. Fitzpatrick fell onto the edge of the shore, and the chubby man let out a yelp. Before he could recover, Noah jumped down the embankment and brought the machete's full force onto his neighbor's neck.

The chubby man's eyes bulged as old man Fitzpatrick's head fell into the water. The current rolled the decapitated head downstream before getting it hung-up on a rock.

Noah stood up straight and tucked a lock of brown hair behind his ear. He backed out of the water and waited for young Hunter (he'd always hated that name) to close in. Once the boy stepped onto dry land, Noah buried the machete in the side of his temple. Hunter dropped to the ground.

Pressing the boy's face into the mud with his boot, Noah wrenched the blade free. Finally, he turned to the man, his eyes wild and chest heaving.

"Thank you. My—my god, thank you," the man said between wheezes.

Noah held up his hand signaling the stranger to be silent. He closed his eyes and listened, but all he could hear was running water and the stranger gasping for breath.

"Just the three?" He asked in a hushed tone.

"Yeah, I think so."

"You think so? This is important."

"They were the only ones I seen."

Noah nodded. Though plump, the man's splotchy skin

seemed loose, as if he'd recently lost a lot of weight in a short time.

Noah stepped into the creek and walked towards Fitzpatrick's head.

"What are you doin'?" said the chubby man.

"He's still…," Noah paused, searching for the appropriate word, "going."

"So?"

Water sloshed over the head as its eyes rolled and its mouth opened and closed. "I can't just leave him like this." He gave the skull a quick chop, ending its motor functions, then returned to the embankment.

"Come on," said Noah, holding out his hand. "That shot will draw more."

The stranger took his hand.

"Noah Barnes," he grunted, helping the man to his feet.

"Alvin Bartlett. Call me Al."

Noah's eyes widened. A Bartlett, he thought.

"You related to Billy Bartlett?"

"Why, what'd he do to you?" Alvin said with a crooked smile.

"No, nothing. I knew him from school. He's a few

grades above me."

"Yeah—my younger brother. Haven't seen him in years though—not any of my family, really," he said with a hint of salt.

"Oh," said Noah, feeling strangely relieved.

In high school the name Bartlett was synonymous with trouble—fights, meth, drinking, bigotry—the real-life Yules of Lyons, New York. To Noah, Billy had seemed like the only civilized Bartlett. He'd broken the mold and lived by his own quirky code of honor. But based on Alvin's bitter tone when he mentioned his family, it made Noah more optimistic that Billy wasn't the only enlightened one.

"We're about a quarter-mile from my house," he said. "Try to keep up."

As they headed towards the Barnes' home, Noah kept lifting his chin, straining to see as far up the path as possible. Alvin had twisted his ankle crossing the creek, causing them to travel at a perilously slow pace—almost as slow as the undead.

When the house, with its empty yard, finally came into view, the knot in Noah's stomach untied.

Alvin noted the boarded-up windows on the first floor.

Set back from the road, a few miles in between towns in either direction, this was an ideal location to weather the chaos. Alvin wondered if his family's home was equally intact, but then quickly thought better of it.

Before unlocking the front door, Noah looked around to make sure no one would witness them entering. The hallway was dimly lit.

Alvin's eyes widened. "You got a generator?" It had been weeks since he'd seen a working lightbulb.

Noah chuckled. "That'd be like a dinner bell that never stops ringing. No. This side of the county ran on hydroelectric power. The hydro plant must still be running on its own," he said. "Enjoy it while it lasts, because I expect it to end any minute."

"You're lucky. I come from Big Weed. The whole town is dead."

"They must be on a different grid."

As they entered the kitchen, Charlie's attention perked up. He charged in from the living room, shotgun in hand.

"Who's this?" he said, holding the gun fast across his chest.

Noah hesitated, surprised by his father's sudden reboot.

"This is Al. I found him cornered in the woods."

"And you brought him back here?" He said with a mixture of disbelief and disgust.

"He busted his ankle. I couldn't just leave him there."

Charlie's eyes fluttered with confusion. He looked the stranger up and down. "He can't stay here," his father declared.

"He needs help."

"We can't be looking after charity cases."

"Dad, he can barely walk. We can't just turn him away. It'd kill him."

His father shook his head.

"You know what mom would say if she could hear you?"

"Your mother isn't here."

"And right now, I'd say that's a good thing. She'd be ashamed of you."

The old man stood eerily still, staring at the intruder in his home. Finally, Charlie looked back at his son, "As soon as he's fixed up, he has to leave," he said and then stormed out of the room.

Alvin and Noah looked to the ceiling as Charlie's

footsteps pounded overhead.

"Sorry if I put you out," said Alvin, wrinkling his brow.

"Don't mind him. This whole thing has got his head all twisted up."

"He ain't the only one."

Noah poured a glass of water from the sink and handed it to his guest.

"Running water too?"

"Well water drawn by an electric pump."

Alvin downed the water as if he were in a drinking contest. "Don't tell me you've got a meat locker in the basement."

Noah laughed. "Yeah, right." He went to the pantry and searched the cupboards. "Limited selection, I'm afraid. I haven't had time to go on a supply run in a while. Beans alright?"

"Anything."

While Noah heated the beans on an electric hotplate, his little sister skipped into the room.

"Daddy said we have a damned stranger in the house!" she exclaimed, excited to see someone new for the first time in weeks.

Noah tilted his head and raised his eyebrows. "Abby, what did I say about lowering your voice?"

"Sor-ry."

"This is Alvin."

"Hello there, little lady," Alvin smiled. "What's your name?"

"Abigail," she beamed.

"That's a pretty name. A pretty name for a pretty little girl."

"Thanks!" She said with a toothy smile.

"Hey. Volume." Noah spoke as if he were shocked she didn't listen the first time. He turned to Alvin. "We speak quietly inside. When we're outdoors we barely say anything, and if we do it's in a whisper." He pointed outside. "Those things like noise."

Alvin nodded. "I'll be sure to follow the rules," he whispered and gave a wink to Abby.

She giggled.

"You can wash up in the bathroom upstairs. I'll fix up the guest room for you at the end of the hall."

"You have hot water?"

"Yup."

"This place is amazing."

"For now. It won't last."

"Did you get bit?" said Abigail.

"Bit? No, but I would have if it weren't for your brother."

"He saved daddy too," she said proudly. Then her demeanor downshifted. "But he couldn't save mommy."

Noah looked at her sternly and shook his head. Abby stopped talking.

"Speaking of," said Noah, changing the subject, "where did you come from?"

"Well," Alvin stopped himself. "Abigail, why don't you go play while your brother and I talk?"

Abigail frowned and clomped into the living room.

"Heh. Cute kid. Reminds me of my own sister." When she was out of earshot Alvin continued. "I've been the gate operator for Lock 17 on the Barge Canal for the last five years. It's a government job—great benefits—decent pay."

"Was," Noah corrected him.

"What?"

"That life is over, man."

"Oh, right," he looked down, pausing briefly, and then

explained the events that led him there.

Alvin had been sitting in the control cabin when a twenty-foot yacht drifted into the lock and slammed into the lower gate. He called to the ship on his bullhorn, but no one responded. Something was wrong. He opened the filling valve and waited for the yacht to rise.

After it buoyed, Alvin hopped aboard and began exploring the ship's deck. It was quiet—empty. When he reached the stern, he spotted a thick trail of blood leading below deck.

"Hello?" he called into the darkened cabin. "Is someone hurt?"

Footsteps sounded, slow and heavy. A chill swept over Alvin, freezing his lungs. The hazy-eyed, bloodied face of an elderly man passed into what little light reached down below. His skin was sallow, and he stunk like roadkill, but Alvin had yet to encounter the living dead, so he didn't know what to make of the man.

He shambled toward Alvin, arms outstretched, his jaw gently rising and falling. As Alvin backed away, he had tried to reason with him.

"But that didn't work. He just kept comin' toward me,

and moanin'. God, those moans…," Alvin said, rubbing his temples, "enough to strip the varnish off a deck. And then his old lady came out behind him. Aside from the man's bloody face, he looked alright. But her," he shuddered. "She was all messed up. Her tits were—just—gone. I mean, like, picked clean. You could see her ribs and everything, man."

Alvin had run to the bow, climbed over the pulpit, and dropped onto the catwalk that ran along the lock's top gate. The dead couple followed. The woman climbed over the handrail, but she fell off the ship and buckled over the catwalk railing like a towel hung out to dry. The old man leaned over the pulpit and swiped at Alvin's head. While trying to avoid his grasp, Alvin lost his balance and fell over the rail into the canal. He rolled beneath the muddy water, bobbing to the surface just in time to see the woman fall in after him. Frantically, Alvin paddled downstream, desperate to get as far away from the couple as possible.

The river bent, depositing Alvin onto a sandbar. He coughed and wheezed as he crawled ashore before flopping onto his back at the water's edge. The river gently lapped at his feet while he tried to catch his breath. He could have laid there for an hour—if it weren't for the screams.

Alvin crawled up the muddy incline toward a small fishing skiff that lay overturned at the crest of the riverbank. Slowly, he peeked over the skiff. He was in a trailer park.

One of the trailers was engulfed in flames, and its blaze was starting to spread to the trailer next to it. The park's residents didn't seem concerned. Instead, they chased each other in and out of the doublewides, tackling anyone who couldn't get away. As Alvin looked over the carnage with utter incomprehension, he heard the rhythmic swishing of water behind him. He turned slowly, somehow already aware of what he'd find.

The old woman from the boat had gotten hung up on the same sandbar as Alvin, and her interest in him hadn't waned in the slightest. As she shambled towards him with water draining through her ribs in fine crimson rivulets, Alvin experienced a total paradigm shift. It was the same shift that everyone who encountered the living dead had gone through: the realization that no person could survive such horrific wounds for more than a few seconds, let alone continue to function unimpeded. These things were no longer human!

Whether or not a person survived their first encounter usually depended on how quickly they accepted this new paradigm, or, as in Alvin's case, just dumb luck. Either way, the odds were not favorable.

Alvin crawled over the skiff and staggered toward the nearest trailer. Two more dead noticed him and began hobbling in his direction. He tried the door, but it was locked. Circling the trailer, he came across a collection of junk stacked against the rear of the home. Alvin pulled a broken lawn chair from the junk pile. He opened the chair and set it beneath a window.

As his pursuers drew nearer, Alvin climbed onto the chair, careful to keep his feet on the metal frame instead of on the frayed webbed seat. Nerves formed a small pit in his stomach. He knew he didn't have the strength to keep running if the window was locked. He gritted his teeth as he pushed on it hard. The latch was resistant, but it gave. Alvin forced the window open and, with his last measure of strength, pulled his body inside the trailer.

He landed on an orange shag carpet at the foot of a bed.

Alvin closed his eyes, took a deep breath and then dragged himself to his feet. Just as he grasped the top rail on the window, a pair of blanched hands lashed the sill. The hands were followed by the head of a young man, no more than twenty years old, with messy blond hair and a pierced nose. One side of the boy's face was caked with dirt and dried blood. He snarled at Alvin, revealing two missing teeth, and then reached for him. But before the boy could grab hold of him, there was a sound of tearing fabric and he disappeared.

Alvin took one last look outside. The boy thrashed on the ground, the lawn chair having closed around his legs like the world's most benign bear trap. Relieved, Alvin closed the window and engaged the latch.

As he surveilled the room, he discovered the body of a middle-aged woman in the bed. On the nightstand beside her sat an empty pill bottle and a half-finished fifth of Jim Beam. The body twitched and Alvin jumped back knocking a framed photo off the wall. He stared at the woman, waiting for something else to happen, but nothing did. Nerves, he thought.

Alvin stepped into the hallway and softly closed the

door. He scanned the trailer. The home was minimalistic, either by choice or financial circumstance. There was a kitchen with a small table and two chairs. In the living area, there was only a worn-out couch sitting in front of an old boxy CRT television. No people, thankfully.

Alvin checked the front door, making sure it was locked. The windows were all out of reach from ground level, but he made sure they were latched as well in case any of those things were smarter than the ones he'd encountered so far. After the place was secured, Alvin rifled through the kitchen cabinets until he uncovered a bottle of Tennessee Williams whiskey. He plopped onto the floral-pattern couch and took a few pulls from the bottle before passing out.

Alvin was awoken the next morning by a distant thumping sound. He blinked at his surroundings. Nothing looked familiar. More thumps sounded in slow succession, and it was then that he remembered what happened the day before. As Alvin stood up, the bottle of Evan Williams fell off his lap spilling whiskey onto the carpet. He stared down the hallway.

Thump… thump… thump.

Alvin swallowed the knot in his throat. He crept down the hall, stopping outside the bedroom, and put his ear to the door. As if the woman could sense his presence, she slammed against the door hard enough to jar his head. Alvin fell back against the wall, cracking the wood paneling beneath his weight.

The woman in the bedroom let out a slow, undulating moan that caused every hair on Alvin's body to rise to attention. It suddenly occurred to him that he hadn't locked the bedroom door the day before—wasn't sure it even had a lock. If the woman simply turned the doorknob, she would be right on top of him.

Alvin flew out the front door of the trailer. The sun was yet to rise, but it was light enough to see more than a dozen of those things lumbering in between homes and on the gravel drive. Their heads perked up, alerted by Alvin's noisy exit.

He ran to the overturned fishing skiff and righted it in an instant. Alvin pushed the boat into the water and a shrill screech sounded as the aluminum hull scraped against rocks and roots. The noise attracted the attention of every corpse in the trailer park, and they all began to swarm. The fresher corpses seemed to move faster than the elderly couple he'd encountered on the yacht.

The young man with missing teeth had apparently escaped the chair-trap and reached the riverbank. He stumbled down the incline and landed headfirst on a rock. Alvin stared, expecting him to get up, but, for some reason, he didn't. As more dead drew close, Alvin moved to the bow and dragged the skiff into the water. He pulled the boat to the edge of the sandbar and jumped inside.

The old woman from the yacht pushed her way to the front of the mob. She stumbled down the sandbar and managed to grab hold of the transom with one hand. Alvin sneered. This woman was his curse. He climbed into the stern.

"Leave me alone!" he said as he stomped on her hand.

He crushed the tips of her index and middle fingers, and with that she lost her grip and sank into the canal. Alvin sat down on the stern seat, never taking his eyes off the ripples that marked his stalker's disappearance.

The current carried Alvin several miles downstream

before he was driven ashore by hunger. He managed to eke out a few weeks in a cabin along the riverbank, but there was little food. Alvin threw his fate back to the will of the canal, which eventually carried him parallel to the Barnes's home. Alvin had climbed through a drainage ditch that ran under the road and tried to get into the house across the creek from Noah's.

"But there were more of those ghouls inside."

"The Fitzpatricks," Noah interjected.

"Huh?"

"The ones chasing you—they were my neighbors. I thought they might have turned. Checked their place a while back. I could hear them moving around inside, but it didn't sound right, and I wasn't about to risk my neck for a few cans of soup. I wonder if their son Adam is still alive. He wasn't with them."

Alvin shrugged. "I didn't think to ask," he said wryly. "That's when you found me." He swallowed the memory along with a heaping spoonful of beans. "I owe you."

"You don't owe me anything, Al. It's what you do in that situation—if you can." Noah saw that his chewing became more labored with every spoonful. "Why don't you go wash up and then rest a bit? You must be exhausted after all that."

Alvin nodded. "Thank you, Noah." He took his hand and gave it a firm shake. "Thank you."

But Noah wasn't paying attention. His head was cocked to the side, the lower eye squinting while the upper widened under a raised eyebrow. He put his finger over his lips.

Silently, he moved to the kitchen window and peered through a gap in the boards. Four dead were milling around outside.

Noah turned back to Alvin and whispered, "They're here for the gunshot." He glanced out the window again. "Don't move. Don't make another sound until I tell you it's ok. They should move on so long as they don't think there's anything here to eat."

Alvin nodded rapidly.

"I'll tell the others."

As Noah crept into the living room, Alvin settled down onto a kitchen chair with only a creak to give away his movement. He couldn't keep his eyes open for more than a few minutes. After that he lay his head on the breakfast table and, within seconds, was fast asleep.

II

Adam Fitzpatrick stood before the altar of the church of Saint Anthony of Abbot. The Roman Catholic church was locally renowned for being made entirely of wood—even using wooden pegs instead of nails. Adam milled around the pulpit aimlessly. He had entered the cathedral to investigate a clamorous noise he heard that afternoon but found nothing, aside from others like him.

A month earlier, Adam was alive—working as a delivery man for Sears department store. He and his coworker, Jason Davies, had pulled into the driveway of a small, two-story home at the end of Lansing Street to deliver a dishwasher to a recently widowed senior. Jason sat in the truck listening to the radio while Adam knocked on the back door. No one came to let him in. Instead, his presence was acknowledged by a low groan, like that of a man in pain.

Adam's EMT training took over. He kicked open the door and rushed inside. The kitchen lights were off. After his eyes adjusted to the darkness, he spotted the old man standing naked in the dining room. Judging by his pale complexion and dazed look, Fitzpatrick guessed he'd had a stroke.

"Are you okay, sir?" he spoke loudly.

The man didn't respond. He lurched toward the boy, mouth agape.

When Adam reached out to steady him, the old man clamped his false teeth on Adam's index and middle fingers, tearing them off with a jerk of his head.

Adam yelled and pushed the old man to the floor. When he examined his hand and saw the bloody stumps that used to be two calloused fingers, he let out a shrill scream.

Fitzpatrick backed toward the door as the old man took to his feet, the severed fingers still rolling around his gnashing porcelain teeth. The octogenarian maniac shuffled toward him. As Adam stepped backward, he tripped on the door's threshold and fell down the stairs onto the concrete walkway, chipping the bone in his left elbow. A wave of pain shot up his arm. Before Adam could recover, the old man stumbled out the door and tumbled on top of him.

Fitzpatrick tried to block his attacks, but the pain left him disoriented, and the old man managed to sink his dentures into Adam's neck. He bit off a mouthful of flesh, and Adam let out a cry.

Jason barely heard Fitzpatrick's screams over the heavy guitar and rapid double-bass of Metallica blaring on the radio. He killed the music and craned his head out the window. Someone had his partner pinned to the ground.

Jason jumped out of the truck to help his coworker. When the old man heard him approaching, he slowly turned his head and let out a gravelly moan. Shreds of Adam's flesh were stuck between his rust-colored teeth. Jason stared into his frosted brown eyes, devoid of humanity. It was an image he couldn't have dreamt up in his wildest nightmares. Jason opened his mouth to speak, but the only thing that came out was a timorous "No." He jumped back into the truck and peeled out of the driveway taking one of the neighbor's sentinel shrubs with him.

The old man continued to feed until the meat grew cold and unappetizing. No longer interested, he moved on to find warm flesh.

Within minutes Adam's body began to twitch. A mild trembling grew to full-on convulsions, which continued for several seconds until, all at once, his body ceased moving.

After a moment of stillness, his eyelids opened revealing a pair of glazed brown eyes. Adam turned onto his side and slowly picked himself off the ground. He let out a long, inaugural moan.

Pistol shots broke out down the street. Adam's head swiveled toward the noise, his mouth agape with excitement. Then he awkwardly shuffled off in their direction.

After a couple hours of exploration, it appeared there was nothing to eat in the cathedral. Eventually Adam and the other corpses slowly staggered down the red-carpeted aisle and out into the gray June afternoon.

Adam stumbled down Church Street like a drunk, not quite aware of where he was going or what he was looking for. He was only aware of a primal impulse originating from the center of his decaying brain, urging him to eat—to survive.

A plastic shopping bag blew across the street. Adam lunged after it. He grabbed hold of the bag and brought it up to his mouth. It took only one bite to realize that this was not food, even though it had moved. Adam let go of the bag and it floated to the ground.

A moan sounded from down the street. It was followed by another moan, and then another, and another. When the call relayed to Fitzpatrick's location, he too moaned and then ambled off in that direction.

Halfway down the street an orange tomcat darted across the road. Fitzpatrick chased after the cat with such focus that he ran right into a black wrought-iron fence. Adam buckled over with enough force that the spear-like tip of one of the posts stabbed into his gut. He let out a visceral groan prompting a few of his brethren to investigate, but they moved on as soon as they saw that no food was involved.

Adam pushed himself off the fencepost. A chunk of his liver remained skewered on the spike. The singular motion of the mob caused him to forget about the cat, and he continued walking down the street in the direction of the other corpses.

This went on for hours—walking, getting distracted, losing attention, another distraction, more walking…. It had been two hours since Fitzpatrick left Saint Anthony's, yet he hadn't ventured more than a mile from the cathedral—none of them had.

At exactly five o'clock, an electronic timer triggered the church's mechanical carillon, creating a long melody of bells, which used to alert the town of evening mass. Every corpse within a two-mile radius heard the sonorous bells, and each one gravitated toward the source of the sound, just as they had twice-a-day, every day since the majority of the town's residents had died.

A half hour later, Fitzpatrick was wandering around the pulpit of Saint Anthony's Church, investigating something he could no longer remember. After a couple hours of exploration, he found there was nothing to eat, and so he wandered down the aisle and out into the cool, evening air, as did the others—hundreds of them.

III

Alvin had been living with the Barneses for almost a month. There was never a formal agreement, but it was understood that Alvin was to help with sweeps and supply runs and etc. in exchange for a room. The arrangement stoked contentions between Charlie and Noah on a near-daily basis. The old man hated Alvin, for reasons Noah couldn't quite pinpoint, and he wanted him gone. Charlie had given his son several ultimatums, but Noah ignored them. He figured he had the final say and refused to turn Al away since it was Alvin who now helped Noah reconnoiter for walking corpses and scavenge the local houses for supplies. He even took to looking after Abby like she was his own sister. Charlie hadn't helped with any of those duties in over a month, and it was nice for Noah to have someone to share the day-to-day responsibilities. Despite Alvin's contributions, his father still found fault with him.

"I want you to take back his gun. That was a special edition," said Charlie one morning.

Noah's soiled fingers tightened around a glass of water. He and Alvin had just returned from replacing a section of pipe on the watermain—took them damn near a month of digging just to find the leak—and he was not in the mood.

He peered through the window to make sure Alvin was still outside smoking a cigarette. "You mean you're going to use it?" Noah responded sarcastically.

Charlie ignored the comment. "He's eating too much of our food."

"He finds most of the food."

"I don't like the way he's always around Abby."

"He's looking after her, dad—something else you should be doing."

"I don't trust him."

"Well, I do, and until you start pulling your weight like you used to, I decide what's best for the family," said Noah.

"Then I will," snapped Charlie.

Noah arched his eyebrow. "Volume," he said calmly.

"I will!"

"Shh!" Noah put his finger to his lips. He eyed his father up and down. Charlie hadn't left the safety of the house in over a month. His father had real fear put in him, perhaps to a phobic degree, and Noah didn't believe he had the nerve to confront it. "Then do it."

"Fine." Charlie's whisper cut through the air like a whip. "And when I do, he's gone."

Noah stared at his dad. "Why do you hate him so much?"

"You know what I think about those Bartlett boys."

"That's it. Isn't it? It's about the family he comes from, not who he is."

"Those boys are rotten fruit—same as their old man. Same as your friend Billy," he added.

Noah shook his head and walked away. If there were a portrait of his father hidden away in their attic, he thought, it had grown quite ugly over the past couple months.

As Noah entered the living room, he found Abigail grimacing from the top of the staircase. There was a large wet spot at the center of her nightgown. When she saw her big brother she began to cry, embarrassed.

"Did you have another accident, Abby?" Although he tried, Noah couldn't conceal the frustration in his voice. It was the fifth time in three weeks she had wet the bed and he was getting tired of washing soiled linen and pajamas. "It's ok, there's no need to cry," Noah said as he climbed the stairs. "It's not your fault."

He went to hug his sister, but she recoiled.

Her consideration surprised him. "It's fine, I've had worse on me. What was it, another nightmare?"

"There was a dead man in my closet," she whimpered.

"The dead men are out there, and we take care of them. It was a bad dream, that's all." He took her hand. "Come on, let's get you changed."

Charlie looked up as the pair headed down the cellar stairs. "What's wrong?"

"An accident—bad dream." He was annoyed by his father's sporadic concern. "You want to help her?"

Their father shook his head. "You're so eager to be the man of the house—you go right ahead and be him."

Noah felt his face turning red. He opened his mouth to launch a cutting diatribe but thought better.

They stood in the basement next to the washing machine. Moisture made the gown cling to Abigail's skin, and Noah had to help her pull it over her head. He threw the nightgown into the washing machine before rooting through the contents of the dryer for something clean to wear.

"Here, put these on," Noah said handing her new

underwear and his old Limp Bizkit t-shirt.

"It'll get ruined," she protested.

Noah chuckled. "It was ruined the moment it was printed."

The shirt came all the way down to her knees. Noah turned his head while she pulled off her underwear and swapped them for the clean pair. As she pulled them up to her waist, she hissed in pain.

He looked at her curiously. "Are you hurt?"

Abigail nodded.

Noah's eyes darted around the room. "Is it painful," he swallowed uncomfortably and tilted his head toward the floor, "down there?"

"A little."

"What does it feel like?"

"It stings."

Noah thought for a moment. "You might have a urinary tract infection. Mom used to get them sometimes."

It looked as if Abigail were about to burst into tears.

"No, no, don't panic," he said waving his hands in front of her. "It's not a big deal. Women get them all the time—guys too sometimes."

"What do I do?"

"I'll get you some antibiotics on our next run. Pills—they'll fix it. For now, you're just going to have to try and put up with it." He paused, considering what else to do. "Why don't you go wait in the bathroom and I'll draw you a bath. That should help. I'll change your sheets in the meantime."

After his little sister had gone upstairs, Noah shook his head in frustration. This was something his mother should have been there to handle. He poured a half-cup of detergent into the washing machine, gently closed the lid, and then started the wash cycle.

Why am I the only person in this family who can keep it together? He thought.

It didn't happen that day or the next, but over the course of the week, Charlie started accompanying his son outside again. He didn't go far at first—only several feet from the front door—but after a few days he moved out into the yard, and then into the backyard, and then out into the woods. Noah could hardly believe it.

Almost two weeks had passed before they encountered

a corpse. The blue overalls that hung from one of his shoulders were spotted with white paint and blood. It stood with its back to them, staring into the branches of a rotting Dutch elm tree.

Probably after a squirrel, Noah figured.

He measured his old man's reaction.

Charlie stood frozen, tightly gripping his shovel. Noah held out the machete and nodded to his father, but Charlie was oblivious. He was breathing heavily, transfixed on the corpse. Noah shook his father's shoulder. The old man snapped out of it. He looked at his son with wide eyes, the color drained from his face. Noah nodded to him more emphatically this time and, after a moment's hesitation, his father replied in kind, exchanging the shovel for his son's weapon.

Charlie looked down at the cutting tool he had once used to carve paths through the woods for his son, but now it seemed more like an alien artifact. Noah waited a moment, and when it appeared that his father couldn't muster the nerve, he took a step toward the corpse. Just then Charlie put his arm out in front of him. He closed his eyes, and in one deep breath the decision was made.

Charlie sprinted. The corpse turned at the sound of rapid footsteps approaching. Its jaw slowly lowered in an attempt to moan, but before it could make a sound Charlie swung the machete at its maggot-riddled head with such force that its body spun around in a circle before falling limp to the ground.

Charlie stood over his kill, panting. Noah walked up beside him and examined his father's handiwork.

"I told you I could do it," he declared bitterly as he traded the machete back for his shovel. His hands shook with adrenaline. "Tomorrow. He goes."

Noah stared at the stiff body beside his feet as his father walked back toward the house with a sense of urgency. "He goes," he said to himself.

IV

Noah tried to break it to him gently, but it was no use.

"You turn me out, you're gonna kill me," he said.

"Aren't you worried about your own family?" asked Noah.

"Would you want to go back to a father who used to beat on you whenever he got drunk? Or a brother who broke your arm when he was tweaked out on meth? My fourteen-year-old sister miscarried last year—we still don't know which one of my brothers did it to her."

Noah swallowed. Rumors about the Bartletts had swirled around school ever since he could remember, but apparently reality had greatly exceeded the legends.

Alvin stared into space. "Christ, you should have seen what dad did to Billy when he found out," Alvin trailed off, and then looked at Noah curiously.

"It's a different world, Al," said Noah abruptly. "People need each other now more than ever. Besides, it's out of my hands."

"I'll bet it is," he said looking toward the living room. He could feel Charlie sitting silently in his recliner staring into oblivion. Alvin lowered his voice. "You'd rather have him around than me? I get food. I clear the wanderers. I look after Abby. He kills one of those things and suddenly he's the house MVP?"

Noah looked down the hall to make sure his father wasn't coming, and then replied in a hushed tone. "It's not that simple, Al. He's my dad. This is his house."

"Sometimes blood ain't thicker than water."

Noah furrowed his brow. What the hell is he getting at? He thought. "Maybe it's different with your family, Al—because of what you've been through. But he's my father. He'll always be my father."

Al shook his head and then walked outside.

Early the next morning Alvin and Noah scurried around packing supplies. Noah stuffed as many canned goods as he could into a canvas backpack. Alvin might be exposed, he thought, but at least he won't starve. Not right away, came an unpleasant afterthought.

Abigail was quiet at breakfast. She sat stirring her oatmeal with a spoon, not saying a word to anyone. In the last few weeks, she had become pickier and pickier about her meals—sometimes refusing to eat at all.

Noah took a break from running around. “Abby, why aren’t you eating? Are you upset because Al is leaving?”

She didn't respond.

“Gonna miss me, aren’t you, sweetie?” said Alvin, feigning a smile.

Abigail nodded timidly.

“I know, but he has his own family to protect,” said Noah.

“There’s no need to lie to her. I already told her why I was leavin’.”

Noah pursed his lips and looked at the ground.

The whole family stood outside to see Alvin off, each Barnes looking on his departure with drastically different feelings. Alvin slung the backpack on his shoulders.

“Here,” said Noah as he handed him their Regal 870 shotgun. “You have seven rounds. Don’t use them if you don’t have to.”

Charlie was aghast at the gesture. He hadn’t said a word while Noah stuffed Alvin’s pack with food. He would have gladly forfeited half of their rations to be rid of him. But giving away one of his guns was crossing the line. “What the hell do you think you're doing? We need that!"

"Keep your voice down," said Noah. There was fire in his eyes. "If we're going to throw him out, we can at least give him a fighting chance."

Alvin smiled. He would have gladly forfeited the gun if it meant seeing Noah put Charlie in his place.

He put his hand out to Noah. Noah took it and pulled him in for a hug, which surprised Alvin. Then he got down on one knee and opened his arms to Abby. She hesitated and then moved in for a hug. Alvin whispered something to her, but Noah couldn't quite make it out.

Alvin stood up and looked at Charlie. "Thanks," he said hollowly.

Charlie stared past him. "Mmm."

Alvin rolled his eyes and then headed down the driveway.

As Noah watched his friend leave, the knot in his stomach grew tighter. Before Alvin disappeared behind the bend in the driveway, Noah called to him.

Alvin turned around, an inquisitive expression on his face.

"Wait," said Noah. He sighed. "I'll go with you."

"What the hell are you talking about?" Charlie seethed through his teeth.

"I can't just stand here knowing that we may be sending him off to die. Maybe you can, but I can't."

Alvin walked back toward the house. "You'd come with me?" he said, incredulous.

Noah nodded.

"You can't be serious?" said Charlie. "What about us? You'd just leave us here unprotected!"

"Calm down. It'll only be for a day—two at most. Besides, you said it yourself, you can do it. That's the reason he's leaving, right? Because you're capable now?"

His father's eyes flitted from side to side as if looking for a response.

"Right?"

Charlie didn't dare renege on what he had said a few days before. Alvin was finally leaving, and he wasn't about to give his son a reason to argue in favor of him staying.

"Yes."

"Then you can handle it."

"But what if a drove shows up while you're gone?"

"A drove? Dad, how many of those things have we seen

lately? One a day? Sometimes less? Back when this thing got ramped up, we couldn't even leave the house. But now? They're dying out."

Noah took an extra hour to pack a bag.

Before they left, Abigail hugged her brother. "Please don't go with him," she whimpered into his ear.

Noah knelt next to her. "Don't you worry. Those deadbeats don't stand a chance against me and my big muscles," he said, flexing one arm.

She didn't laugh.

Noah kissed her cheek. "You take care of daddy for me while I'm gone."

Abigail began crying. She ran inside.

He frowned.

"She'll be alright," said Alvin.

"Yeah." Noah nodded. "Let's get going."

As Alvin started down the driveway Charlie put his hand on Noah's shoulder. His son turned to him, and Charlie could tell by the way he crossed his arms that he was preparing for an argument.

"Look, I know I can't stop you. I just want you to be

careful." Charlie's face softened—warmed almost. "Come back to us, will you, son?"

Noah smiled. He hugged his father for the first time in months. "I promise I'll come back. Alive," he added with a grin.

The pair headed down the driveway and across the road. There were no corpses in sight and, aside from the buzzing of cicadas, all was quiet. Even after being cut off for so long, Noah still found the silence eerie.

"We should find a car," said Alvin.

They weren't more than two minutes into their journey and already Alvin was proving that he desperately needed Noah's guidance.

"No. Too loud. We'll take your boat and paddle down the canal until we get to town. We'll walk from there. The boat will keep us out of reach of any nearby dead."

"That'll take forever. Why don't we just take a car instead?"

"It's not worth the risk. The dead are like magnets. Each one you come across starts following you—and moaning. Others hear that and come crawling out of the woodwork. Before you know it, we'll be dragging along a horde of those things like we were the Grand Marshals of a goddamned zombie parade."

"But we can outrun them in a car."

"Yeah, but what if we break down or come to a roadblock? When something catches their attention, they don't let up. We're better off taking our time and staying off the road."

Alvin sighed in concession.

They headed over a wooded embankment, across a set of railroad tracks, and down a slope of ballast. The boat was beached on the muddy shore a quarter mile upriver right where Alvin had left it. They pushed it into the water and climbed in.

The boat rocked from side to side under their weight. Alvin held his arms out, awkwardly trying to keep his balance.

"Take a seat," said Noah, trying not to laugh. He pulled out an oar from beneath the bulwark stay and pushed the boat away from shore.

As they rowed down the canal, the sun peeked through smoky stratus clouds. Birds sang and occasionally a carp leapt out of the muddy water in pursuit of a fat bug, and for a moment, Noah forgot that they were heading into the heart of a cannibal village.

The leisurely cruise illusion was shattered, from a distance, when a disheveled onlooker waded into the water in the direction of Noah's and Alvin's boat. Fortunately, the only harm it posed was to Noah's peace of mind; when the water reached its chest, the current swept the man off his feet and he disappeared beneath the murky ripples.

Noah sighed. He wondered if a semblance of normality would ever return in his lifetime. Would they all eventually decompose into harmless piles of bones, or were enough living people still around to replace their dwindling ranks for decades to come?

After passing beneath a bridge clogged with abandoned cars, they came to the local marina. Unlike more urban marinas, with elaborate networks of quays that can berth dozens of boats, the Lyons marina had a single retaining wall running along the shore to which boats could be moored. Most of the vessels were gone except for a fifteen-foot sailboat and a thirty-foot yacht named Serenity. Black smoke wafted from Serenity's cabin.

"We should take that boat," said Alvin pointing at the

yacht.

"Are you kidding? That would attract way too much attention. Besides, judging from the smoke, the engine's shot."

"No, I mean the dinghy."

Noah eyed an inflatable raft hanging off the upper deck of the ship. It was outfitted with a small electric motor, which was probably quiet.

"Is it worth the risk though? That's what you have to learn to ask yourself."

"This is taking too long. If we don't go faster, we risk not making it into town until dark, and I don't think we want that."

Noah covered his mouth with his fist and thought for a moment. "Alright. Let's go for it."

They paddled toward the boat launch. The skiff beached on the cement incline with a scraping sound that sent a chill up Noah's spine. Off to a great start, he thought.

Alvin climbed over the bow followed by Noah. They crept up the ramp and onto the promenade. Despite the marina being deserted, Noah felt uneasy. There were several derelict motorhomes and cars, as well as a gas station with a little café—plenty of nooks for something to pop out of.

As they made their way to the yacht, Noah noticed a Winnebago parked on a hill, gently teetering from side to side. He decided not to mention it. If one of those things were still inside, it must be trapped, or it would have gotten out a long time ago.

The yacht looked to be derelict, although they couldn't really see through the cabin's tinted windows. Noah hopped onto the side deck and took a few steps toward the stern. He turned back when he realized Alvin had yet to come aboard. Noah gestured for him to follow, but Alvin didn't move. He stood frozen with his arms across his chest.

"What's the problem?" Noah whispered.

Alvin trembled. After a moment, he stuck his foot out as if he were about to come aboard, but his boot stopped over the gap between the boat and the retaining wall. He looked at Noah.

"I—I can't," he whispered shaking his head. "I can't get on." He backed away breathing heavily.

Noah had seen that same look of paralyzed stupor

before, on his father, and then he remembered the story Alvin had told him the day they met. His first encounter with the dead happened on a yacht like this one.

Noah thought he could get Alvin aboard with a little coaxing, but why waste the time and risk the sound of a conversation. "It's alright," he said, trying to tamp his frustration. He had long since grown tired of coddling behavior that put him at risk. "Get back in the rowboat and swing around her stern. I'll meet you there."

Alvin nodded in agreement. "I'm sorry."

"Don't worry about it. Just go."

Alvin headed back to the skiff.

Noah climbed onto the upper deck. As he made his way around the cockpit, he held his shirt collar over the bridge of his nose, trying not to breathe in the black fumes rising from the deck lounge stairwell below.

The dinghy was suspended by davits over the stern of the ship. Noah looked around for some kind of release lever but couldn't locate one. He stared at the dinghy, about to give up, when he felt a sharp pain in his shoulder. Noah howled and wheeled around, reflexively flailing his arms at the source of his pain. A burnt corpse fell back against the ship's helm. Noah gasped. The thing was so badly charred that it was difficult to tell whether it had been a man or a woman. Noah's blood dribbled down its chin, the red liquid contrasting sharply against its blackened flesh.

The thing got up and limped closer. Noah cupped his shoulder. As he stepped backward, his heel stubbed the lip of the deck, and Noah fell over the railing into the dinghy.

Seconds later the corpse was on him, snapping at his face and neck. Charred skin flaked onto Noah's face as he fought against it. As he turned his head from side to side to avoid its snapping jaws, he spotted a crank on the backside of the ship. Noah kicked it hard, sending the handle spinning like a pinwheel in a strong wind. The dinghy plummeted into the water below, striking the surface at an angle. The momentum of the fall flung the corpse out of the boat and into the canal.

Noah lay propped against the rubber gunwale, stunned by the impact. From the corner of his eye, he could see Alvin paddling toward him.

"You alright?" he asked as he neared. "What happened?"

Noah propped himself up on his elbows. "There was a zo—."

But before he could finish his sentence, Alvin cocked an oar over his shoulder like a baseball player about to swing for the fences. Surprised and confused, the only thing Noah could do was duck and cover his head.

Alvin swung the oar over Noah's body, cracking the skull of the burnt creature as it tried to pull itself into the raft. Its moan turned to gargles as it sank back into the murky water.

Noah scrambled to the other side of the boat. "That's what happened."

Using the oar, Alvin pulled the raft against the skiff.

He talked as he transferred their guns and packs into the dinghy. "Damn it. I should have gone with you. This wouldn't have happened if I didn't chicken out." Then he climbed into the raft, his heft and maladroitness causing him to nearly fall over the opposite side.

"I shouldn't have gone in the first place. It's stupid to take a risk if you don't have to," he said, hoping to subtly ingrain the guideline into Alvin's brain. "I just," he said and let out a nugget of laughter. "I was getting so sick of paddling."

Suddenly there was a large splash a few feet away as another corpse fell into the canal.

"Dead dummies," Alvin said with a smirk.

Noah looked around the marina. The clamor was enough to rouse the dead from every nook and cranny within earshot. A half-dozen weaved through the maze of cars on the bridge. A few more came out of the back of the Dockside Cafe, and another came stumbling out of the public restroom near the launch. The one that had fallen in the water a moment before came bobbing up to the surface like a buoy, flailing and twisting only a few feet away from them.

"Jesus!" said Alvin, leaning away from it.

Suddenly a sharp screech sounded from the Winnebago. Their heads pivoted like chickens in its direction. The formerly teetering motorhome had begun slowly rolling toward them.

"What the hell?" said Alvin.

"Something knocked it in gear," Noah replied. "We have to get out of here, now." He turned his attention to the electric motor and attempted to glean its operation.

Black and red wires hung from the bottom of the motor. He connected them to a battery in the stern.

"Will it work?"

The Winnebago was picking up momentum. In a moment, it would be right on top of them.

"It has to."

He flicked the switch on the tiller and a power indicator flashed. They both breathed a sigh of relief. Noah switched the motor into reverse and twisted the throttle on the tiller handle. The little two-horse outboard pulled them out of the path of the Winnebago seconds before it drove off the retaining wall and slammed into the water.

"Yeah!" Alvin punched the air.

Noah tried to smile, but it looked more like a pained wince. He looked over his shoulder. The motorhome was sinking nose-first into the canal. Too many close calls, he thought.

Hauling the weight of two full-grown men was a strain on the small motor, but it was still a far more efficient method of travel than paddling. And, to Noah's surprise, the engine made less noise than the oars did when they banged against the gunwale after each row.

When they were far from the marina, Noah stopped the boat and switched positions with Alvin so that he could tend to his shoulder.

"So why could you get in this boat, but not in the yacht?" said Noah.

"Because I can see everything in this boat."

"Got it." Noah pulled his collar over his shoulder and examined the bite. Blood oozed from the oval teeth-marks.

Alvin's jaw gaped open as the color blanched from his face.

Noah scooped up a handful of water from the canal and poured it over the wound.

"Does that mean you're gonna turn into one of them things now?" Alvin asked nervously. His hand instinctively reached for the paddle.

"Bites won't kill you—not necessarily."

"But in the movies people always turn after one of those things bites 'em."

"It's not like it is in the movies, Al. We already have the disease. It won't kick in until I die, and I'm not going to let a scratch do me in."

"What do you mean, we already have it?"

"I knew someone who died without having been bitten, and she came back anyway."

"Who?" Alvin asked skeptically.

Noah hesitated. "My mother." He took a deep breath. "She slit her wrists—no bites—and she still came back."

Alvin's eyes widened. This was the first time Noah had mentioned his mother. He wasn't big on unloading his personal baggage. "I'm sorry." He didn't say anything for a moment. "Can I ask what happened?"

"I don't know. We woke up one morning and she was gone." He sighed. "I guess she just got tired of it—tired of being scared and nervous every minute of every day." Noah stared into the water. "You know how I told you about my father losing it after one of those things surprised him in the shed?"

Alvin nodded.

"It was my mom." Tears welled in his eyes. "I had to kill her. The old man, he," his voice caught in his throat. "I think once he saw her, he was ready to go too."

Alvin swallowed.

A moment of silence passed between them, and then Alvin said, "But how do ya know for sure a bite won't trigger it?"

"Common sense." Wiping his tears away he turned back to Alvin. "If I had rabies, why would it take a bite from a rabid dog to trigger what's already in my blood?"

From the look on Alvin's face, Noah wasn't sure he understood.

"I told you. It's not like the movies."

V

Noah and Alvin arrived in Lyons around noon, or so Noah surmised based on the sun's position in the sky. After pulling the boat onto the shore, they gathered their packs and guns and headed east, in the direction of Alvin's house, on the far side of town.

The two cautiously crept through the streets, scanning for threats as they moved. Alvin was surprised by how clear the roads were. There were some bodies lying around of course, but none of them were reanimated. Maybe what Noah had said about the chaos dying down was more truth than smoke, he thought.

Noah found the complete dearth of living dead to be very suspicious. Based on the diminishing frequency he had encountered at his home, he had hoped their ranks were thinning. But down to nothing? His stomach twisted with anxiety.

They stopped at the intersection of Commerce and Cyprus Streets. A Walmart loomed in the distance. Noah tapped Alvin's shoulder and then pointed at the superstore.

"But is it worth the risk?" Alvin asked, mimicking his friend.

Noah smiled. "I need to get to a pharmacy, and you need supplies."

Alvin shook his head.

"You don't know what you'll find at home. Your family could be out of food." Noah looked around. "Besides, if you've been on the outs with them, don't you think arriving with a big bag of supplies would be quite the peace offering?"

Alvin had a pained look on his face.

"We'll be ok," Noah reassured him. "We just have to be smart about it."

Noah looked down the five-lane commercial drive that bisected Lyons. Aside from a peppering of abandoned cars and the occasional carcass, he could see clear to the other end of town. There was no movement anywhere. How's that possible? He thought. There had to be at least a few dead wandering around.

Something tugged at Alvin's pant leg. He gasped and jumped back. A desiccated, male corpse reached for him. Its pelvis was twisted backwards relegating it to locomotion by dragging.

Noah buried his machete in its skull.

Alvin put his hands on his knees and caught his breath.

"If that's the worst we encounter today, I'll consider us lucky," said Noah as he stepped on the corpse's neck and extracted the blade.

Alvin looked up just in time to see the traffic light shut off. "That's weird. The light stopped working."

Noah squinted at it. "Maybe the power grid finally shut down."

Alvin smirked. "Your old man's probably freaking out right now."

Noah looked at him askance, but the glance went unnoticed by Alvin.

They crossed the street and weaved between the pumps of a gas station that stood at the end of the Walmart parking lot. Along with half a dozen cars, a large fuel tanker had been abandoned there. It sat above the underground fuel tanks, unable to deliver its liquid cargo.

There were still more than twenty cars in the lot. Noah took an odd comfort at the sight of a corpse thrashing around in the back of a silver Nissan. Just seeing anything move made the otherwise total lack of activity slightly less unsettling.

With the power off, Walmart's automatic doors refused to open.

"Grab one," said Noah.

Each man took hold of a leaf and pulled until the doors slowly spread apart. As they came to the inner door, Alvin readied himself to repeat the process, but Noah held out his hand.

"Hold on," he whispered. Cupping his hands to the glass, he peered inside. The soft sunrays streaming through the frosted skylights were enough to give him a dim view of the front of the store. Movement. "There's a few trapped inside," Noah said, not taking his eyes away from the glass.

Alvin peered through the window. Several bodies shambled through the aisles, which were littered with merchandise, without any apparent thought or purpose.

Noah chuckled sardonically. "It looked like this before everything went to hell."

The joke was lost on Alvin. "Should we go in?"

"We should try to lure them outside. There could be as many of them inside as there are cars in the lot."

"How we gonna do that?"

"We'll figure something out."

They left the entrance and walked around the building. In the back was a loading dock with two huge metal garage doors that sat four feet above the ground. One was closed, but the other was ajar by a few inches. Silently, they both wondered what horrors might lie behind such a large and ominous door. Perhaps a hibernaculum of undead to counter their uncanny good luck walking through town?

Placing his palms against the bottom slat, Noah lifted the door. At first there was nothing, but then, out of the darkness crawled the corroded body of a young man. Alvin and Noah leapt backward, startled. The boy reached over the edge of the dock, exposing a deep bite on his forearm. He pulled himself under the door, and then fell onto the pavement with a crack. He tried to get up, but Noah stopped him with a quick swipe from his blade.

They waited to see if any more would follow. After some time passed, Noah climbed onto the dock's edge and threw the door open. It retracted with a clatter, flooding the loading bay with sunlight.

The center of the loading bay was mostly empty, aside from a few boxes strewn about the floor. The sides of the bay were lined with large racks stacked with various goods in cardboard boxes, and at the far end of the room was a barricaded set of double doors.

"We need to lure the ones inside through this door," Noah said looking down at Alvin. "While they're piling up out here," he pointed at the boy, "we'll go in through the front and seal the doors from the inside."

Alvin nodded.

Noah walked to the rear of the loading dock. A handcart stacked with boxes of air conditioners blocked the doors. The kid—probably a stock-boy or cashier—must have holed-up in the backroom before dying from his wound. Noah unlocked the wheels and pulled the cart out of the way. Suddenly, a car alarm started blaring, and he nearly had heart failure.

He ran back to the edge of the loading dock to find Alvin struggling with the door of a locked car. Noah started to ask what Alvin was doing when the door behind him swung open and a fat woman in a polka dot dress shuffled through. He raised the machete, but before she could cover half the length of the dock a lanky man in a navy-blue jumpsuit joined her. And then, the door shuddered as it thumped against a third corpse.

Damn it, thought Noah. This could be bad.

He jumped to the ground and ran towards the front of the store, waving for Alvin to follow as he darted past. Alvin looked into the loading bay. Dead were filing out the back door like endlessly spawning enemies in a video game. He forgot the alarm and ran after Noah. After rounding the corner of the building, they stopped to catch their breath.

"What the hell did you do?" asked Noah.

"I was looking for something to draw them out and set off the car alarm." He chuckled, clearly embarrassed. "Sorry."

Noah peered around the corner. A small group was already pounding on the car. Another corpse fell off the dock, then picked itself off the ground and joined them. "Well, you got their attention. Let's get inside before any more come out of the woodwork."

They circled around front and entered the store's foyer, closing the doors behind them. Before passing through the second set of doors, Noah peered toward the gas station at the end of the parking lot. No movement.

A mile east of Walmart, a horde of corpses lumbered in the streets surrounding Saint Anthony of Abbot Church. Out of the hundreds of bodies, only one heard the faint honking in the distance.

Fitzpatrick moaned, triggering a succession of guttural groans from the other corpses nearby, which spread out further like ripples in a pond. He headed in the direction from where the sound emanated. The dead in his immediate perimeter followed, as did the dead in the secondary perimeter, and the tertiary, and on and on. In only a few minutes, every cadaver in the area was following Fitzpatrick toward Walmart. The mass of bodies shambled down the streets and, with the power no longer running, there was no carillon to call them back to the church.

Noah and Alvin split up with the intention of clearing out any stragglers before focusing on scavenging supplies. As he crept through the store, Noah couldn't stop thinking about the car alarm. It would continue to blare so long as those mindless things kept bumping against the vehicle. But that car must have been sitting in the same place for months, Noah thought. It will have to die soon.

He was close to the back door when an old man in a

gray wool suit lurched toward him. Noah stepped aside, allowing the suited man to fall forward. While he struggled to pick himself up, Noah sunk the machete into the back of his skull.

Dragging the dotard by the collar of his suit-jacket, Noah passed through a pair of swinging doors marked Staff Only and made his way down a dimly lit corridor. The only available light was beaming through porthole windows on the doors at the end of the hall, which led out to the loading dock.

Nearly twenty corpses pounded on the screaming car. Far from an endangered species, thought Noah. Thanks to the cover of the siren, he was able to roll the body off the dock and close the garage door without any of the dead noticing.

Noah returned to the store and stealthily swept through the rest of the aisles. He finally found Alvin among the section of rotting produce. A little girl in a white Sunday dress was slowly walking toward him. Other than her glazed eyes, she looked unspoiled. Noah watched Alvin with curiosity. Instead of bashing her head with his bat, he backed away. The little girl came within a foot of Alvin, but before she could land a bite, Noah darted at her, lodging his blade into the side of her head. She dropped onto the cool, tiled floor with a light thud.

"What were you doing?" said Noah, wide-eyed with bewilderment.

Alvin breathed heavily. "I—she," he stuttered, "she looked like my sister."

Noah looked at the girl. Her curly brown hair evoked a slight resemblance of Abby, whom Alvin had said also looked like his own sister. "She's not your sister. None of these things are anyone anymore. You have to keep telling yourself that."

Alvin swallowed and nodded.

"The store seems clear, but be careful. Grab what you need. I have to get antibiotics—for two people now," he said, nodding at his blood-soaked shoulder. "I'll meet you at the entrance in a half hour."

"Yeah. Sure."

As Noah headed toward the pharmacy, Alvin knelt next to the little girl and smoothed her hair over the fresh gash on the side of her skull.

Noah ducked beneath the pharmacy bar flap, blade

extended in front of him. He believed that all the corpses had been rooted out of the store, but he knew better than to take anything for granted. Despite almost a complete lack of cognizance, the dead had a strange knack for surprise.

Noah pawed through the medicine bottles looking for any drugs with names ending in "-cillin" or "-mycin." Although not thoroughly looted, the shelves had already been picked over enough to indicate that Noah wasn't the first person to come in search of medicine. Whoever else had been there was most likely pounding on the car in the backlot now.

After dressing his wound and swallowing a few Amoxicillin capsules (the same antibiotic he was prescribed for acne when he was 13), Noah went in search of the sporting goods department to scavenge for ammunition.

As he rounded an aisle leading back to the produce section Noah stopped, frozen in disbelief. Alvin was kneeling next to the dead girl, his hand rooting beneath the skirt of her dress. His other hand was in the crotch of his unbuttoned pants.

"What are you doing?" Noah said, not entirely sure what

he was seeing.

"What?" said Alvin surprised. His hands snapped back into the open.

"What are you doing!"

"Nothing. Nothing," he said, springing to his feet. I was just—I was seein' if she had anything useful on her."

"In the skirt of her dress?"

Alvin's face flushed. "No, I—I just—I meant—"

Noah shook his head. "You are messed up, man."

"Oh, come on." He opened his arms, trying to entreat his friend. "You said it yourself, these things ain't people anymore."

"You just said she looked like your sister! And now you're—" Noah abruptly shut up. His eyes widened as a whirlwind of memories spun around inside his head before falling into a coherent line: Abby's despondency, her loss of appetite, the nightmares, the bedwetting, her pelvic pain, and at the end of it all: Alvin—always eager to watch over her.

Noah's mouth opened, but no words came out. After a moment, he finally spoke. "Dad was right," he said to himself. He pulled his machete from its sheath and pointed it at Alvin. "You get away from her!"

"Hey now, Noah, relax. She's dead!"

"I don't care! She was a little girl," he said, his voice catching in his throat, "and I'm not going to let you defile her!" He stepped toward Alvin.

He put his hands up in the air. "Come on, man. You know how long it's been since I seen a woman?"

"That's not a woman!" He looked away, thinking of Abby, and then looked back to Alvin. "Did you touch her?" There was a hint of desperation in his voice.

"What?"

"My sister, did you touch her?"

"Of course not, buddy." Alvin said, forcing himself to chuckle. "I would never. She's like my own sister."

Noah kept the machete pointed at him. "Yeah. I know how the Bartletts treat their sister."

Alvin looked away.

"Who really got her pregnant, Al? Was it you? Or are your brothers just as sick as you are?"

The blade was now so close that Alvin could see the bits of dried blood stubbornly clinging to the scores in the metal. It made him think of an old war movie he had seen as a kid where fighter planes were plastered with kill markings on the sides of their fuselage. His lips quivered, but he said nothing.

Noah sheathed his blade. Disgusted he turned and headed toward the front door.

Alvin followed him. "Hold on now," he said putting his hand on Noah's shoulder.

Noah rotated his arm, shaking off his grip.

As they exited the first set of double doors Noah froze, startled by what lay outside. A drab sea of living dead was spreading across the parking lot like a barrel of spilt tar.

"Look, we gotta—" Alvin's words were muffled by Noah's hand covering his mouth.

"Shut up," Noah whispered. He headed back into the store pulling Alvin along with him.

Once inside, they closed the second pair of doors.

"Oh my god. What are we gonna do? What are we gonna do!" said Alvin as he stared through the glass.

"Volume." He strained to see through both sets of doors. Hundreds of living dead were headed their way. Where did they come from? He thought. Where the hell were they hiding this whole time? "Calm down. They're coming for the alarm, not us. The car’s battery should die soon. As long as we don't do anything to draw their attention they should leave once they find there's nothing to eat—most of them anyway. So until then, just stay away from the doors and don't make a sound.”

“Yeah. Yeah, good thinking, buddy.”

Noah sneered. “This doesn't change anything between us. We're stuck here, for now, but after that, you're on your own.” He started to walk away but then turned back to face Alvin. And if I get home and I find out that you did something to Abby, I’m coming back for you.” He pointed at Alvin. “Do you hear me? I swear to god, I will come back.”

VI

It was dusk when Adam Fitzpatrick reached the gas station at the end of the Walmart parking lot. By then the car alarm had stopped. His glassy eyes shifted toward the highway that ran beside the store and disappeared over a hill into the vermilion horizon on the edge of town. He stared long and hard at the road. It looked inviting—almost familiar.

Adam broke from the mob and shuffled toward the highway. A few undead took notice and followed him. They, in turn, attracted their own followers and so on like a chain of magnets pulling iron stragglers. By the time Fitzpatrick made it to the intersection, he had thirty acolytes in tow. Thirty escorts to accompany him home.

Alvin and Noah didn't see much of one another throughout the rest of the day. Noah spent his time scavenging, organizing and reorganizing supplies, discarding some things he now doubted as useful, and picking up other items he had overlooked. Alvin was lurking somewhere, Noah knew, but he didn't care where so long as the creep stayed away from him. Noah was thankful he would only have to see Alvin once more, at daybreak. They had agreed that it would be best to leave the store together before going their separate ways.

As the light from the skylights dimmed, Noah lay back on a faux leather recliner atop an elevated furniture display. He sharpened his machete on a mill file he'd found in the hardware department. What would he really do if Abby confirmed his suspicion? Could he really kill another man, a living man? He wondered. The only thing keeping him from snapping into a rage was the naïve optimism that Alvin was telling the truth. Perhaps he really hadn't touched Abby, and the little girl in the produce aisle was the result of some undeniable, deviant urge brought on by months of celibacy. Either way, Alvin's perversion had unleashed a revulsion in Noah that could never be undone.

Noah awoke the next morning to an alarm bell of paint cans toppling onto the floor a few aisles away. He bolted upright and the mill file fell onto the stage, making a clunking noise.

The sight of a corpse shuffling down the aisle confused him. He was about to hop down and kill it when he noticed another one further down the aisle. Noah looked in the opposite direction. Three more were headed his way.

"Damn it," he said to himself.

Noah grabbed the rifle and slung his backpack over his shoulder. He crept across the display, weaving between the furnishings. He snuck past the three that were heading toward him before hopping off the shelf and darting into the corridor that led to the loading dock.

Perhaps if it weren't so early, if Noah hadn't been groggy and confused, then the soft glow of dawn coming through the round porthole windows at the end of the hallway would have signaled that something was wrong. But for whatever reason or combination of thereof, Noah forgot that he'd shut the garage door the day before.

As he pushed open the doors of the loading bay, his heart jumped into his throat. The garage door was wide open. The car alarm was silent. Three corpses meandered around the platform, and at least thirty more aimlessly milled about outside. They moaned and advanced. The pack of living dead on the ground also took notice and some of the fresher corpses began climbing onto the loading bay.

Noah's breathing sped up as he took a few steps

backward. He ran back down the corridor into the store. As he pushed open the doors, he was surprised to find six corpses there to greet him. There were too many to take out with the machete, not without risking a pile-on. Noah put the rifle to his shoulder and shot the nearest two in the head. As the echo of gunfire faded, it was replaced by a cacophony of moans and the arrhythmic clomping of shoes throughout Walmart. They were everywhere.

Terror seized Noah. He spun around and ran back into the hallway with the dead close in tow. At the other end of the corridor, the three corpses had already pushed through the loading bay doors. He took out the first few that entered, but as soon as he shot one another filed in. If that weren't enough trouble, the door leading back to the store creaked open as more dead entered.

Noah ran to the center of the hall, establishing a fifteen-foot buffer zone in both directions. His hand trembled as he pulled a box of rifle rounds from his pants pocket. A few shells clanked against the tile floor as he hastily reloaded. Noah looked to one end of the hall and then the other. Throngs of dead were closing in from both sides, their ranks growing so thick that they blotted-out the light coming through the doors.

His fingers tightened around the grip on the rifle stock, imprinting the hand-etched crisscross pattern into the meat of his palm. A variation of this moment had haunted his dreams many times before, and each time, after waking up beaded in sweat, he vowed he would never let those things eat him alive—not if he could help it.

Noah swallowed hard. With one hand on the forestock and the other on the grip, he awkwardly positioned the rifle muzzle beneath his chin. In his dreams the dead moved like a slow-burning fuse, and he always had time to reflect, but, in reality, the moment was unfolding too quickly. And maybe that was better. He took a deep breath. Three… two… one, he counted in his head. "I'm sorry, Abby."

Just as he was about to press the trigger, Noah caught sight of a spherical shape protruding from the wall a few feet away. A doorknob. He moved the muzzle away from his chin and tried the knob. It wouldn't turn. Noah aimed the rifle at the latch and fired. The door inched open.

Noah darted inside and slammed the door. The entry led to a large storeroom that had been converted into a makeshift office. Beside the entrance stood a green file cabinet. Noah pushed it onto its side, barring the door.

Muffled moans sounded from the hallway as the door began to thump against the cabinet. With so many dead congregating outside, Noah knew the barricade wouldn't buy him more than a minute or two. His head frantically pivoted around the room. A dead man sat at a desk in the corner. Blood was splattered on the wall behind him, and a revolver hung from one crooked finger. Although the body hadn't moved, this was no time for a surprise. Noah immediately put a bullet in its sallow forehead, and the corpse jolted like a marionette that had its strings tugged.

At the far end of the room, a metal staircase led to the roof. Noah sprinted to it and began to climb. Halfway up the stairs, he heard the screech of the file cabinet scraping against tile as the door was forced open. Two dead spilled onto the floor and were immediately trampled by the hungry mob that followed. Noah didn't look back. He ran to the top of the staircase and threw open a scuttle hatch.

The white gravel covering the expansive roof made it look like a desert dotted with skylight domes and secondary HVAC units. The only thing Noah could find to weigh down the hatch was a five-gallon bucket of roof sealant and a wooden chair. Better than nothing, he thought, setting the objects on the hatch.

He ran to the nearest roof-edge and peered over the side. It was at least a twenty-foot drop to the ground. There wasn't much time, but a broken leg would only guarantee he'd be torn to pieces. That'll be plan B, he thought. Noah jogged the perimeter of the store looking for another way down. As he made his way around the roof, he could see the undead wandering for miles in every direction.

He skidded to a halt, kicking up loose gravel. "No." A dreary parade of corpses stretched down the road running in the direction of his house. "No!"

The roof hatch shuddered, startling him. Noah kept moving. His priority to survive was irrationally replaced by the need to get home. The dead moved slowly. Maybe, if he were fast enough, he could make it back in time to protect Abby.

At the front of the store, Noah discovered a pitched roof. The bottle redemption center had been tacked onto the main building a few years after the original store was constructed. It still left a ten-foot drop to the ground, but that was a height Noah could walk away from, assuming he didn't thoroughly botch the landing.

The chair-weight fell off the hatch as the bucket of sealant hopped up and down. It wouldn't be long before they spilled onto the roof like ants fleeing a flooded colony. Noah looked over the parking lot, which was now a minefield of undead. He was trying to devise a route to the gas station when suddenly the sealant bucket was thrown clear and the dead began climbing through the hatch.

Noah held his breath, and with his pack in one hand and his rifle in the other, he jumped down to the redemption center. He slid down the blue tin roof and dropped onto the sidewalk below.

His feet stung when they smacked hard against the cement, but there didn't seem to be any real damage. The corpses in the parking lot began walking toward him. He raised his rifle and strategically picked off a few. Any dead that hadn't noticed him before were certainly alerted to his presence now.

Noah bolted toward the gas station, weaving between pairs of reaching arms like a running back on the gridiron. Adrenaline seemed to slow time, yet speed up Noah's reactions. In what felt like an instant, he was at the gas station looking for a functioning automobile.

Car after car had either no keys or was perilously low on gas, and with each failed attempt the dead drew closer and closer. The last vehicle was an enormous gas tanker truck. Noah reached up and opened the door. A writhing corpse fell out of the cab and onto the ground. Noah stumbled backwards, but he was steadied by a teenaged boy in a green, pinstriped baseball uniform. The boy grabbed him by the shoulders and mouthed his upper back, trying to find a piece of anatomy protrusive enough to lock his jaws onto. As Noah tried to pull away, the former truck driver wrapped his arms around Noah's leg.

With the number of dead within arm's reach, he knew that if he were taken down now, he'd never get back up alive.

He grabbed the boy by the wrists and doubled over, judo-flipping him onto the truck driver. The boy flattened the driver, causing his arms to splay out.

Noah stepped on the boy's chest, caving his ribcage, and leapt onto the truck's running board. He swung his body into the cab, and no sooner had he closed the door than myriad fists began pounding to get in.

Noah sighed, first in relief and then again in defeat once he saw that the key was not in the ignition. He looked out the cab's window for the driver, who most likely had the key, but there were so many corpses clustered outside that he couldn't find him anymore. Noah's chin fell against his chest. Deflated, he stared vacantly at the rubber floor mat. Then a smile slowly spread across his face. He reached down and grabbed an object glinting faintly in the shadows. A keychain.

"Yes!"

His hand trembled as he inserted the key into the ignition and turned, praying that it would be simply too ironic for a gas truck to be out of gas while sitting in front of a gas station.

Fortune finally gave back. The engine roared to life.

Noah breathed a sigh of relief. He shifted the clutch and put the truck into gear. It jerked forward, startling him. He pulled out of the station and onto the furthest lane of the main highway, heading back in the direction of his family. As he passed the super store, he noticed that the front doors were open.

"Alvin." He spoke the name as if it were an obscenity.

The road leading to the Barnes' house was dotted with undead, but the tanker was powerful enough to mow them down with minimal resistance. The truck's transmission was similar to the standard transmission on his old car, but for some reason Noah couldn't get the rig moving over thirty miles per hour.

During the seemingly endless drive home, it began to drizzle. Noah repeated a prayer. "Please be ok. Please be ok."

There was a break in the density of bodies on the half-mile stretch of highway leading to Noah's house. His heart fluttered. Had he passed the front of the horde? He wondered.

The truck was too big to navigate up his winding driveway. Noah stopped the rig in front of his mailbox, which had been snapped-off at the base and pushed into the drainage ditch. He left the engine idling in the road, jumped out of the cab, and ran up the driveway.

Noah stopped short at the sight of his family's home. The front door was kicked-in, and a few corpses milled about outside. Hunched silhouettes passed across sections of windows where the boards had been torn off. The baritone moans of what sounded like a couple dozen corpses droned from inside the house like a beehive. But there was no gunfire. No screams. No signs of life.

His stomach turned, and his body began to teeter from side to side. She could be locked in the attic—or the basement, he thought, still unwilling to give in to the obvious. Dad would have stuck her somewhere for me to find, if he had any sense left in him.

There were far too many to kill. Noah's eyes narrowed as if searching for an idea somewhere in the distance, and, after a moment, he spotted it.

He ran back to the truck. A few frontrunners to what remained of the second half of the horde were already within throwing distance. Noah hopped into the cab and grabbed his backpack. After unbuckling one of the straps, he tied it around the pull cord that hung from the ceiling and let it drop. As the pack dangled, the air-horn let out a loud, steady belch. Every corpse within a mile radius perked up at the sound of the horn. Noah jumped down from the cab and slammed the door.

He skidded down the ravine in the direction of the canal, stopping beside the mouth of the drainage pipe that ran beneath the road. Noah slowly plodded through the pipe, careful to keep his splashing to a minimum. He stopped at the far end and waited in the shadows. Eventually a steady line of dead streamed down the driveway, eager to investigate the noise emanating from the road. When the flow of corpses tapered off, Noah climbed the streambank and ran up the driveway.

With machete drawn he flew through the front door. The kitchen looked like it had experienced an earthquake. The breakfast table lay on its side with two of its legs knocked off, and the matching chairs were trampled to pieces. Broken cans of food were strewn about the floor, liberated from their shelves by blasts of buckshot that blew the cupboard doors right off their hinges. The acrid scent of burnt gunpowder mixed with the aroma of preserves and the all too familiar stench of rotted flesh.

Noah stepped over a faceless body before entering the living room. There he found a few more bodies with pulp for faces, but no Charlie or Abby.

He moved upstairs. There was a hole in the wall outside the first bedroom, which was the guest room where Alvin had stayed.

Dad switched to slugs, thought Noah. He was running out of ammo.

Peering through the hole he saw a man and a woman hunkered over his father. They tore chunks of flesh from his body like hyenas feeding on a zebra carcass in a nature documentary. The shotgun lay beside Charlie. Several spent shell casings were strewn about the rug, along with three motionless corpses, their heads reduced to unrecognizable stumps by close-range gunfire.

Noah dashed into the room. "Hey!" He blurted.

The corpses turned their heads but didn't attack. Their current meal still warm, they went back to eating. It was the first time Noah had gotten the attention of the undying, only to be promptly ignored again.

He charged, swinging the machete with such force that it decapitated the first corpse's head clean off. The headless body knocked into the woman and pushed her onto her back. Before she could recover, Noah plunged the blade through her torso so hard that it pinned her to the floor like an insect tacked to a setting board. She pulled at the blade, managing only to mutilate her hands and nothing else.

Noah stood hunched over his father's mangled body, shoulders slowly rising and falling as he regained his breath. There's nothing left, he thought. Nothing. Tears rolled down his cheeks and fell onto his father's neck.

Suddenly his father coughed spraying blood over his chest. Noah's mouth gaped. He knelt beside Charlie and took his hand.

"Dad?" His voice creaked.

Charlie's eyes fluttered open. He squinted at his son, as if trying to place a face he hadn't seen in years. "Y—you shouldn't have left," he said between shallow gasps of breath.

Noah winced. "I know. You were right about Al. I didn't see it." He closed his eyes and shook his head. "I protected him."

His father nodded slightly, and then his eyes rolled into the back of his head. The blood that pooled in his bite wounds lessened as his heart grew weaker. Charlie's grip tightened and then relaxed.

Noah cupped Charlie's hand and closed his eyes, trying to reflect on his father's passing, but the incessant snarling from the pinned woman was too distracting. Noah stood.

He placed his foot on the woman's ribs and yanked the machete out of the floor, only to plunge it right back into her forehead.

He looked back at his father again. Charlie's body twitched. Suddenly, a high-pitched scream sounded from down the hall.

She's alive! He thought.

Noah pulled out the blade and dashed into the hallway. He burst into his sister's room where he was surprised to find Adam Fitzpatrick pounding on the closet door.

"Adam?"

Fitzpatrick turned. His bug-eyed gaze and bobbing jaw resembled the face of a ventriloquist's dummy.

"Get away from her!"

Darting forward, Noah swung the machete at Fitzpatrick's head, but at that moment Adam lunged beneath the blade, tackling Noah.

As Noah slammed against the hardwood, his machete fell and clattered against the floorboards. Adam grabbed Noah's shoulders and leaned in for a bite. Noah palmed Adam's face with one hand and groped blindly for his weapon with the other. He could feel the edge of Adam's teeth as they repeatedly grazed the meat of his hand.

Noah grunted, "You want it?" And in one quick, fluid motion he stuck his fingers into Adam's mouth, cupping them over his lower teeth, and pulled. Before Adam could bite down, Noah dislocated his jaw from the base of his skull. Adam fell onto his side giving Noah the opportunity to scramble for his machete.

Noah got to his feet. He raised the blade over his shoulder.

Adam sat up. He touched his lower mandible, which sagged awkwardly. When he tried to close his mouth and could not, Noah thought he registered a faint look of confusion. Noah cared little to examine it, however, and lodged the blade into the side of his neighbor's head. Adam's animation ceased immediately, as if he were a mechanical toy that Noah had just switched off. Fitzpatrick fell to the floor, never to move again.

Noah hobbled over to the closet.

"Abby. Are you in there?" He called through the door.

"Noah?" Abby replied in a muffled voice.

"It's me, sweetie. You can come out. I got him."

The closet door opened slowly, and Abigail stepped out.

Her bloodshot eyes contrasted sharply against her pale skin as they nervously scanned the room.

"Oh, thank god," Noah whispered. He squatted and pressed her to his chest. "I thought I'd lost you."

Holding her out by the arms, Noah inspected Abby. She pressed a stuffed tiger against her forearm. It was soaked with blood.

"Oh no," Noah's voice quavered. "No. Abby?" he said choking back tears.

She collapsed into his arms.

"No, no, no. Not you too." Tears welled in his eyes.

"I wasn't quiet enough," she whimpered.

He pulled her to him. Her small body felt so weak and fragile in his arms. "No. It wasn't your fault, sweetheart. It was him."

Noah picked her up and sat her on the bed. "Let me see," he said, gently peeling the tiger off her arm.

Abby winced. The bite was deep. Blood pooled in the cavity with every beat of her little heart. Noah yanked off a pillowcase and wrapped it around her arm.

Abigail slumped back on a pile of stuffed animals and began to shiver. Noah took the sides of her quilt and wrapped them around her like a crepe.

"Did Alvin do something bad to you?" said Noah.

Abigail nodded her head gravely.

Noah pressed his eyes shut and turned his head away, as if he were about to be given an inoculation with a particularly large needle.

He turned back to her. "Why didn't you tell me?"

"He said he'd let the bad men in if I did."

His anger flared, but, as he looked at the light fading inside her eyes, the emotion was quickly overpowered by heartache. "I let you down," his voice cracked. "I let you down so bad."

She laced her fingers between Noah's. "He's good at lying."

"I'm so sorry, Abby. I should have been—"

"Daddy?" said Abigail, looking past her brother.

Noah's eyes widened as the color drained from his face. He turned to find his father, hazy-eyed and riddled with bright-red bite craters, teetering in the doorway.

Charlie reached for them, but strangely he didn't advance. He seemed to be stuck at the threshold of the door. Perhaps, in a far corner of his mind, a smoldering ember of memory kept him from attacking his own children.

Noah's eyes glanced at Adam. The machete was still lodged in his head. He stood up and took a deep breath. "I'm sorry," he said, inching toward Adam's body. "I'm sorry I let him in. I'm sorry I left."

His father tilted his head.

"And I'm—I'm sorry for—" He glanced back at Abigail as she bled to death. Noah wiped his tears with the back of his bloodied hand. "Just—everything."

Charlie moaned and stepped toward him. In a flash, Noah leapt onto Adam's back, freed the machete, and swung the blade into his father's temple. Charlie dropped to his knees and then slowly fell onto his side.

Noah turned back to Abigail. Her hands were butterflied over her nose and mouth.

"Don't look at him." Noah sat in front of her, blocking the view of the mangled bodies. "That wasn't daddy. You know that."

Abigail's breath was fast and shallow. Her eyes opened and closed slowly. "Will I be like daddy?"

Noah caressed her cheek. "No, darlin'. I'll stop it from

happening—after you go to sleep."

"I don't want to sleep."

"But you'll get to see mommy—and daddy. And everything will be like it was before —just somewhere else. Somewhere nicer."

"But not you."

"I'll be there soon."

Abby's eyes slowly closed for the last time, like slipping into a deep slumber she had been fighting hard to ward off.

He began to cry. "I love you, sweetie."

"I lo—," she mumbled, and then she was gone.

As he walked across the yard Noah dabbed his eyes with a red bandana before wiping the blood off his machete. From the hill that overlooked the highway he had a clear view of the fuel tanker. Although the horn had run out of compressed air, almost two-dozen corpses were still poking around the truck, looking for the belly in the clam.

Noah flicked the machete into the overgrown grass. It stuck in the ground like a dart in a cork board. He pulled out a box of tracer rounds from his shirt pocket and loaded three cartridges into Charlie's Sedona rifle. Taking aim at the massive, cylindrical fuel tank, he fired.

A reddish streak of burning strontium trailed in the wake of the tracer round. The bullet winged a corpse in the shoulder, spinning her in Noah's direction.

The high-caliber gun kicked like a horse. "Argh!" He cried, doubling over as the pain ripped through his arm. The near-continuous surge of adrenaline pumping through his body over the past couple days had allowed him to forget about the bite on his shoulder.

More dead turned in time to see Noah stand and reload. They shuffled in his direction, but they were too slow. Switching shoulders, Noah awkwardly fired again. The incendiary round pierced the tank and ignited the gasoline. The rig exploded in a huge fireball, incinerating the surrounding corpses. The dead that eluded the fire were killed as well, their brains turned to mush by the blast's pressure-wave.

"Now die!" shouted Noah.

A cadaver on the edge of the blast radius stumbled around, engulfed in flames. Noah smiled as it flailed its arms and then fell onto the ground to writhe and cook.

He dropped the rifle and headed for the toolshed.

Charlie and Abby's graves would need to be dug quickly as the commotion was sure to attract more attention.

VII

Noah barreled down a back road in an Olympic blue Ford truck. A pack of Marlboro's sitting on a bed of coins in the center console caught his eye. He picked up the pack and thumbed the lid open. It was nearly full.

"What the hell," he said.

Using his lips, Noah pulled a cigarette from the iconic red and white box. He pushed the knob on the truck's electric lighter and then slipped the pack into his shirt pocket. When the knob popped out, he pulled it from the dash and pressed the glowing red coils against the tobacco. Noah took a long, satisfying drag and then let out a series of coughs from deep in his lungs. It was his first cigarette in over a year. He used to smoke a pack a day until Abby learned about the harmfulness of cigarettes in school. After that, she embarked upon a crusade to end her big brother's smoking habit, which she successfully accomplished after only a few months of relentless nagging. She had even made him sign an agreement promising that he would never smoke again.

The road was clear until he reached the cemetery. A man in his seventies wearing a soiled gray suit stumbled into the street from behind a small mausoleum, attracted to the truck's rumbling engine. Noah punched the gas and aimed straight for the gray-suited man. His body bounced off the truck and flew into a drainage ditch.

As the truck cruised along the hillside that led past Noah's old high school, a tall corpse wearing a green and white Lyon's basketball uniform stepped into the road. They collided, but instead of plowing him aside as he had the man by the cemetery, the former athlete slid up the hood and crashed through the passenger-side windshield.

Startled, Noah jerked the steering wheel. The truck swerved onto the road's shoulder. He corrected the wheel and had almost regained control of the truck when the corpse suddenly came-to and began thrashing around. With his attention divided between driving and fending off the gangly basketball player's flailing arms, Noah lost control of the vehicle. The Ford tore through the guardrails and rolled onto its side. It tumbled down the hill and crashed into the side of the school's cafeteria, punching a hole through the brick wall.

Slowly, the world came into focus. Noah hung upside down, suspended by his seatbelt. The corpse that had been lodged in the windshield was gone, but now another one was trying to slip through the broken passenger window. Stuck between the cafeteria floor and the door panel, she swiped at the air, just inches from Noah's head.

"Jesus!" said Noah when he saw the girl. Her lips had been chewed off revealing the bloodied bottoms of her gums, and there was a gash on her forehead that went all the way down to the bone.

He unclipped his seatbelt and fell onto the roof. The girl hissed. Noah lightly tossed the machete and rifle through the driver-side window before dragging himself out of the truck. He labored to his feet and performed a brief skeletal inventory. Despite feeling like he just got off the Scrambler at the Barrel County Fair, nothing seemed broken.

Halfway up the hill, the basketball player lay on his back, his pelvis crushed, feebly waving at the languid sky. Noah considered finishing him off but then reconsidered when he noticed several twisted faces appearing in the windows of the cafeteria. More would come from outside the school.

As Noah headed down Smoke Street, he came across his former high school chorus teacher, Professor Hendrick. His dried intestines hung from his gut, dangling over the crotch of his black slacks like the purse worn over a Scotsman's kilt. Noah waved without thinking, but then caught himself and lowered his hand. Hendrick had the slow, rigid gait of someone who had been long-dead—probably since the very beginning. Noah sidestepped his old teacher with ease, but he hadn't gotten more than a few paces before stopping. Hendrick had taught Noah to sing, had believed in him enough to even give him a solo in the high school chorus recital. His teacher deserved better than to be left a slave to his insatiable hunger. Noah turned back, and with one precise swipe, he put the professor down.

Couldn't I have run into any of the assholes I went to school with? Noah thought as he wiped the blade on Hendrick's pant leg.

His encounters with the dead became more and more frequent the closer he got to the center of town. Noah thought about what he had told Charlie before he left with Alvin, "They're dying out. You can handle it." How stupid he had been. This was nowhere near over.

Desperate to get off the street, Noah headed up a dirt road leading to Oakwood Park. The park was deserted, as it had always been even before the outbreak. He and his friends used to spend Saturday nights drinking on top of the "tall hill" that overlooked the JV football team's practice field. The height afforded them a clear view of the road for times when bored police officers would come looking to bust balls. Whenever that happened, which was rarely, Noah and his friends melted into the surrounding trees until the cruiser hung a U-turn and drove out of sight. Even when the police did spot an underage drinker, the steepness of the tall hill was usually enough to dissuade most cops from giving chase. The ones with too much enthusiasm—usually rookies trying to prove something—would typically sprint about halfway up the hill before turning back to the squad car, wheezing in defeat. The living dead, however, would not be thwarted by fatigue. Noah had seen enough writhing bodies floating face-down in the river to know that the dead didn't need oxygen—didn't need to breathe at all.

How was that possible? he wondered. The undead were anaerobic, like cancer cells. Maybe the dead returning was something that happened throughout history whenever life became too abundant. So many ancient civilizations mysteriously deleted from a short meter of history: the

Egyptians, the Mayans—hell—the dinosaurs. These sudden disappearances were always theorized as the result of diseases, famine, meteors, etc. But Archaeologists never looked to the dead for a culprit. Even where some cultures were known to have interred their deceased in vaults or heavy sarcophaguses, or had the remains cremated to harmless ash—these practices were always regarded as unique traditions and nothing more. Maybe they were just cultural customs; or, maybe they were precautions.

With the image of a zombie t-rex in mind, Noah climbed the tall hill. When he reached the top, he headed down an overgrown path that cut through the woods. Although nothing crossed his path during the two-mile trek, he occasionally heard movement. The dead were like sloths. They were drawn to the sound of Noah slogging through the undergrowth, but they were so slow that they were always several steps behind.

The trail let out on Irving Hill Drive, about a mile from Alvin's house. Noah headed downhill, eventually coming to a short, stone bridge running across the Hydraulic Canal.

The Hydraulic Canal was a small waterway dug in the mid-1800s to supply waterpower to the town's many textile mills. In the 1970s, the town connected to a larger hydroelectric power grid several miles away, obviating the need for the canal. It was drained not long after. Since then, it had quietly served as a metaphor for the town's economy.

Noah could walk through the hydraulic and eventually come up right alongside the Bartlett property—easy—but when he looked over the bridge's cement balustrade, he discovered half a dozen dead milling about the dry riverbed.

They must have wandered in through a break in the fence and gotten trapped, he thought. Not that they would see it that way. The canal was a no-go, but he could still cut through the backyards alongside it to avoid the roads.

Noah climbed a wooden fence surrounding the yard of a white, split-ranch home. He skirted an in-ground pool filled with fetid water and a body wrapped in a painter's drop cloth before climbing another fence.

On the far end of the neighboring yard, a man stood with his back to Noah, staring into a toolshed. Noah crept through the tall grass taking care not to give away his presence. As he raised the machete overhead, he paused. He looked the man up and down. There was no blood or wounds on his jeans or denim jacket. Was he alive? Noah wondered. With machete still poised to strike, he snapped the fingers on his free hand. The man slowly turned, and Noah gasped at the steak-knife jammed into his eye-socket. Before a moan could slip between his receded lips, Noah brought the blade down on his head. His body slowly tipped over like a cut tree.

Noah stared at the corpse. Whoever stabbed him was unlucky. Judging by the angle of the knife handle, the blade had slid just beneath his brain. A mere ten degrees would have made a terminal difference.

Something small and dark had slid out of his shirt pocket. Noah bent down and retrieved a Zippo lighter with Rush's Roll the Bones album cover detailed on the face of the matte black case. He pulled the Marlboros from his pocket and lit a cigarette. Without meaning to, Noah made an unsettling comparison between smoking a cigarette after sex and smoking one after killing the living dead.

"Gross," he muttered.

Curious, Noah peered inside the shed. He found a lawnmower, gas and oil cans, and gardening tools—nothing of interest to either living or dead, or so he would have thought.

After cutting through several more backyards, Noah finally reached Lake Avenue. As he crossed the street he spotted a few meandering bodies down the road—far enough away to ignore, for the moment. Noah stopped at the end of the Bartlett's driveway. He unslung his rifle and loaded the magazine to capacity. A machete worked well against the dead, but the Bartletts would probably balk at a large knife. He cycled the bolt and then headed down the gravel driveway.

Noah stood at the foot of the porch, examining the dilapidated colonial home. Its yellow paint had all but peeled off, giving way to its wood paneling, which was gray from years of exposure.

Noah scooped up a handful of gravel and tossed it at the house. The pebbles clattered against the front door. After a moment, he thought he saw one of the curtains shudder. A minute later the door cracked open.

"You livin'?" said a raspy voice. "Say somethin' if y'ar."

"Of course I am."

The door opened revealing Jimmy Bartlett, eldest of the Bartlett brood. He wore a ratty white t-shirt with equally ratty blue jeans. The jeans, like his beat-up Carhartt boots, were splotched with paint of every shade.

A small, red-haired girl peered out from behind him. She looked about twice Abby's age, leading Noah to presume that this was the sister Alvin had mentioned. He had said that Abby reminded him of her, but as the girl cowered behind her big brother like a frightened rabbit, Noah saw no resemblance. Abby was fearless. Or at least she was until Alvin got to her, he thought.

"What do you want?" asked Jimmy. "We ain't got any food."

"Did Alvin make it here?"

He crossed his arms. "Maybe."

"How many of your family survived?"

"Not enough."

"If Alvin is here, send him out. I have business with him."

"And what's that?"

"It's personal."

"You got business with one Bartlett, you got business with all of 'em."

Noah's brow narrowed. His lips pursed. "He…," Noah

hesitated. It was difficult to verbalize. "He touched my sister and got me away from my family. They're dead because of him."

"If he didn't kill 'em, then he didn't kill 'em." Jimmy spat chewing tobacco onto the lawn. "As for your sister, I don't give a damn who Al shacks up with."

"My sister was seven years old, you inbred hick."

The girl recoiled behind her big brother. Jimmy lowered his eyes and shook his head. "God damn-it, Al," he muttered.

"Yes, god damn-it, Al. Now send him out."

"You don't have to worry about him. We'll take care of it."

"No. I'm the one he has to answer to. I'm the only one who can hold him accountable for what he's done."

"I said we'll take care of it. Now you just wander back to wherever it is you came from."

"There's nothing to go back to! Don't you get it?" Shouted Noah. "He destroyed everything! And I'm not leaving until I settle it."

Just then Jimmy was brushed aside by his younger brother, Dakota, who strode up to the edge of the porch with a Remington 870 shotgun in hand. Dakota jerked his head back, whipping his long black hair out of his face, and aimed the gun at Noah.

"He said get! Ya hear? Now go before I put a wad of buckshot in yer ass!"

Noah took a step back. "If you chase me away now, you'll regret it."

Dakota fired. A patch of grass a few feet from where Noah stood jumped into the air.

"Jesus, Koty!" said Jimmy. "You're gonna bring 'em all here!"

Noah backed away. The Bartletts were notorious for being a lawless brood, and that was back when there was actual rule of law. Who knew how far they would go now that any punitive threat was virtually nonexistent.

"You've made a mistake," Noah said before retreating.

"No, you made the mistake, ya damn fool!" Dakota shouted after him. "If I see you again, I'll kill you!"

The last thing Noah heard was Jimmy tell Dakota to shut up before dragging him back inside the house.

Noah was breathing heavily when he got to the end of the driveway. His body trembled with adrenaline and anger.

Alvin was in the house and they were protecting him—he knew it. But how could he beat them now? He had forfeited the element of surprise, and they were protected inside their home.

Moans sounded from nearby. The dead that had been meandering at the end of the street were now close—drawn by his noisy exchange with the Bartletts. Noah dispatched them in seconds.

I should have just let the Bartlett's deal with them, he said to himself. The thought gave him pause. Noah looked to the rusted fence that ran along the bank of the Hydraulic. A crooked smile spread across his face.

He bolted, disappearing into the nearest backyard.

Alvin lay in bed with his back propped-up on a pillow. His body wrenched as he tore into a coughing fit. When the coughing subsided, he winced in pain and gently rubbed the bandage, which had been improvised from an old bedsheet, affixed to his side.

Suddenly the door was kicked open, startling him. Jimmy plodded into the room, his face burning red.

"Still can't keep your god-damned hands to yourself,

can you?" he yelled.

"Wha—what are you talking about?" Alvin wheezed.

"That family you stayed with? They had a little girl? Seems you forgot to mention that part of the story."

Beads of sweat began to grease Alvin's forehead. "What—who?"

"Some little punk just showed up, talkin' about how you crossed him."

Alvin's eyes bulged. "Noah's alive?"

"Yeah, he was just here."

"Come on, Jim, you—you're gonna believe some stranger over your own brother?"

Jimmy sniggered. "If you hadn't done it before, I might not."

The floorboard creaked. Jimmy turned around to find his sister standing behind him.

"Brandy, get out of here! We're talkin'!"

She ignored his warning and came closer. "Do you think that boy's gonna come back, Jim?" her voice quavered.

"I said get out!" He shoved her.

She took a few steps backward before falling onto the floor. Brandy scowled. She stood up and ran out of the bedroom.

“What's she mean, ‘come back’?” asked Alvin. “I heard a shot.”

“He's after you, Al. Koty scared him off, but he swore he’d be back.” Jimmy smoothed his hands over his scalp. Despite being only 35, the top of his head was almost completely bald. “Hell, half of me wonders why I don’t just let him at you.”

“He ain't— gonna—” Another serial of coughs prevented Alvin from finishing his sentence.

“It don’t matter,” said Jimmy dismissively. He pulled a faded blue bandana from his pocket and threw it at his brother. “He's weak. Same as the rest of ‘em.”

As Jimmy walked out of the room, Alvin put the handkerchief over his mouth and cleared the phlegm from his throat. When he pulled the rag away his eyes widened. There was a dark red stain on the white paisley pattern. His hands began to tremble.

Just then the door creaked. Alvin looked up to find Brandy peeking at him from behind the door.

They stared at one another not speaking. Finally, Alvin broke the silence. “You come to make your big brother feel better?" He said, forcing a smile.

Brandy kept an eye on him as she slowly pulled the bedroom door shut.

Alvin frowned as the light from the hallway eclipsed. Then he broke into another coughing episode.

VIII

Noah was kneeling in the shed, tilting a red gas can over an old Coca-Cola bottle. The gasoline swirled around a funnel before draining into the mouth of the bottle. When the glass was three quarters-full, Noah put the can down. He grabbed a rag looped around the handle of a Valvoline container and stuffed it into the mouth of the bottle. Then, he threw the rifle over his shoulder and headed for the bridge on Irving Hill.

Noah approached the fence that surrounded the Hydraulic Canal. A few corpses milled about inside.

"Hey," he whispered. But they didn't respond. Noah looked around, making certain he was alone on his side of the fence. "Hey," he half-yelled.

The dead moaned, tantalized by the sight of live meat. They clumsily scaled the canal bank. The first one to reach him clawed at the metal fence as if he thought he could eventually tear through it.

Noah didn't retreat; instead, he examined it closely. This was the first time he had ever been able to get a good look at a reanimated corpse for more than a few seconds.

It was a man with gray skin and glazed eyes—standard

traits of the living dead. The variables: large chunks of flesh torn out of his arm and an entire swath of skin scraped from his side, exposing part of his ribcage. The jagged point of a broken radius bone stabbed through the flesh on his forearm. It sounded like wood when it grated against the chain-link fence. Noah assumed the break had occurred after the body had died, since there was little blood at the puncture site.

As he drew closer, the thing began to hiss. It tore at the fence with more rapidity.

"I hate you," he said gritting his teeth. "I hate you."

Another corpse approached, falling into the one that was already there. The fence billowed, and Noah stepped back.

"Alright. Let's go."

As he walked along the canal, he dragged the dull side of the machete across the fence. Each body he came across was immediately drawn to the racket. Some dead even came at him from the backyards on his side of the fence. Each time one neared, he hastily split its skull and then kept moving. Noah feared letting the dead in the canal congregate for long. Their numbers were mounting, and he knew a mob that size wielded considerable power.

The sun was setting by the time Noah reached the dead-end of Lake Ave. By then, the collection of living dead in the hydraulic numbered well over a dozen.

Noah moved near the fence and as he did the mob grew more ravenous. The chain-link mesh pushed toward him with an extreme curvature. He could hear bones breaking in the bodies at the front of the mob as the weight of their brethren pushed into them—almost pushed through them. Steel screeched as the section of fence folded forward until it kissed the pavement.

Bodies spilled onto the street. Noah's heart beat rapidly at the sight of so many grotesque figures creeping toward him. If a group that size ever got ahold of him, they would tear Noah limb from limb in seconds. Despite the adrenaline overload, he stayed close. He couldn't just run off in a panic—not if he wanted to direct the mob.

Noah led the group to the top of the driveway and then sprinted ahead. While the dead took time to catch up, he pulled the zippo from his pocket and lit the fuse of the Molotov cocktail. Noah ran up to the house and threw the gas-bomb at the Bartlett's front door. After the bottle shattered, splattering the porch with liquid flame, he sprinted into the backyard.

Dakota had been in the kitchen eating tuna fish straight from the can when he heard something slam against the door. As he ran to the front of the house, he could see flames licking the transom window above the entrance. Dakota grabbed a coat and flung open the front door.

"Jimmy, get out here! We got a fire!" He whipped the flames with the coat. So focused on the fire was he, that he failed to notice the undead drove shambling up the driveway. But they noticed him.

A moment later, Jimmy ran onto the porch with a large jar of water. He noticed the dead immediately.

"Jesus, Koty, there's a whole mess of 'em!" He said, pointing down the driveway.

Jimmy threw the jar of water on the fire and then pulled his brother inside, locking the door behind them.

In the shadows beneath the drooping branches of a huge Norway spruce tree, the glow of a cigarette ember intensified as Noah took a drag. Shots had broken out not long after he ran into the backyard. Round after round, the firing went on for what felt like hours. And just when it seemed like it was over, a final battery sounded, like the grand finale of a fireworks show. If any family in Lyons were prepared for a last stand, it would have been the Bartletts, thought Noah.

While waiting for the dead to clear the house for him, Noah wondered what would be left when they were through. He hoped that Alvin would be alive—maybe locked in some closet, like she was—but he knew that was hoping for much. There was a far greater chance Alvin would be a thriving corpse by then, but there was nothing Noah could do about that. Alive would be ideal. Dead: enough. He could work with either state so long as the brain was intact.

Noah's thoughts were interrupted by a nightstand crashing through an upstairs window. A moment later, Jimmy dropped from the second floor, landing on the lawn at an awkward angle. He was quick to get up and continue moving, which was fortunate, as a corpse tumbled out the window right after him and fell head-first onto the spot where Jimmy had landed.

As he limped into the backyard, he caught sight of

Noah.

"You," he said bitterly.

"Yeah, me," Noah replied holding the rifle up to his shoulder. "Other way," he said, motioning with the barrel.

Jimmy kept coming.

Even though the gun was already loaded, Noah slid out the bolt and locked it back in place for effect. "You take the road or a bullet," he told him. "I really don't care."

Jimmy stopped. His lip curled as he leered at Noah. Then he turned and hobbled away. "I'll get you," he said looking back over his shoulder. "I'll get you."

"No, you won't."

As Jimmy departed, Noah trained the barrel on the back of his head. Why let him live? He thought. Revenge, as he well knew, was a highly motivating emotion. It's likely, Jimmy will come for me when he's ready, just like I came for Alvin.

Noah's finger tightened on the trigger, agonizing over his options until it was too late. Jimmy disappeared around the bend in the driveway, and Noah lowered the gun. It won't matter after tonight anyway, he told himself.

IX

By dawn most of the dead had wandered off. Noah took care of the few that strayed into the backyard, but most had instinctively walked out the front door and onto the street.

When the house looked like it was kicked, Noah quietly slipped in the back door. He crept through the house, stepping over rigid bodies without incident, until he came to the living room. A corpse laid adjacent to a staircase, its head moving from side to side—teeth clicking lightly.

Noah moved in for a closer look. His spinal cord had been blown out through its sternum. Paralyzed, it stared at Noah, futilely biting in his direction. Noah shuddered. If only we had such persistence in life, he thought. And with one solid chop to the temple, its teeth stopped clacking.

With machete drawn, Noah slowly advanced up the staircase. When he reached the landing, Dakota stepped out of the shadows.

Noah gasped. "Jesus."

The skin on his chest and abdomen had been ripped off. His mangled guts dangled beneath his ribcage like the tentacles of some Lovecraftian monster. The flesh on his face had been gnawed off to reveal red-stained facial bones beneath. The only way Noah even knew that it was Dakota was by the black mane that still wreathed his bare skull. Even to a veteran of gore, like Noah, the gruesome sight of Dakota was enough to make his stomach turn.

His eyes now scraped sockets, Dakota could not see his prey, but he could hear it. He stepped forward and stumbled down the staircase. Noah held the broad side of the machete blade in front of his chest, bracing against Dakota's weight as he pinned him against the wall.

Dakota snapped his jaws from side to side searching for a sweet spot. Noah pivoted and heaved his weight against the blade, pushing the horror down the staircase. Dakota glided over the stairs and landed on the floor with a hollow thud. After only a moment's pause, he sat up and turned his head from side to side, listening for Noah. But the only noise he heard was the sip of the machete cutting the air as Noah jumped down the stairs, and by then it was too late. Dakota let out a feeble gurgle as Noah split his head down the center like a Venus flytrap.

Upstairs all the doors were open and the rooms devoid of anything animate, except for one. Noah cupped his ear to the door and heard movement. With machete poised to strike, he kicked the door open and waited, expecting something to spring forth from within. But nothing did. His eyes adjusted after a moment, and he could see a vague shape squirming in the far corner of the room.

As he inched his way into the darkness, the stench of rot grew more pungent. Noah moved to a window on the far wall and tore down a sheet that had been tacked to the frame. The early morning sun filled the room with a sallow glow. In the corner lay Alvin—now a member of the living dead. His brothers had tied his arms and legs to the bedposts with rope. Bloodied bandages dressed his chest and arms. Alvin's wounds were skin avulsions—craters in the tissue that required surgical intervention, but without any hospitals or medical knowledge, the Bartlett's could only slap bandages on their brother and hope his body would take care of the rest.

Noah approached the bed slowly, wary that the ropes might snap at any moment. Alvin thrashed violently, riled at the sight of warm meat.

He held the rifle muzzle up to Alvin's face. "Do you recognize me?" he said.

Alvin moaned and wrenched in his bonds.

"Do you remember what you did to my sister? To my family?"

Alvin stared at him with what Noah hoped was the same glimmer of recognition his father had shown back in Abby's bedroom.

"I could have protected them." He thought of the horde that had overtaken his house, and how there were so many dead—perhaps too many to fend off. "I—I would have thought of something. I always do." He paused. "But instead I was with you."

Noah slung the rifle over his shoulder and unsheathed the machete. Gripping the handle with one hand and the pommel with the other, Noah pushed the blade into Alvin's shoulder. The tip stopped at the scapula. Noah looked into his eyes hoping to see even a faint register of pain, but Alvin's only response was his snapping jaws. Noah turned the handle and again watched Alvin's reaction. Nothing. Nothing but all-consuming hunger.

Noah dislodged the blade and stepped back. He rubbed the bridge of his nose. Was revenge now impossible? He wondered. He looked back at Alvin, who was still relentlessly trying to bite him, when he had an idea—one that could have been torn straight from the pages of Dante's Inferno.

Noah raised the machete overhead and chopped down on Alvin's arm, hacking at the elbow again and again until he had completely severed the forearm. He put his foot on Alvin's chest and, with one swipe, cut off the hand on his other arm, just below the restraint. Noah turned the blade over as he raised the machete above Alvin's head. He swung the blunt side down on Alvin's mouth, breaking his jaw and knocking out most of his teeth.

Noah stepped off Alvin's chest and admired his handiwork. The newly-mangled Alvin made feeble biting motions with his destroyed mouth as he continued to reach out with one limbless arm. A wicked grin spread across Noah's face.

A floorboard creaked behind him. Noah wheeled around, the machete arched over his shoulder ready to strike. "Drop it!"

Brandy opened her hand, dropping a carving knife. The tip of the dinged-up blade stuck into a wooden plank.

Noah looked her up and down. "How did you—?" Not get devoured was what Noah was thinking, but his shame wouldn't let him finish the sentence. If she had been killed, it would have been his fault.

She didn't answer immediately. "I'm good at hidin'," she said, averting his gaze.

Noah didn't know what to say.

"You gonna use that on me?" she said timidly.

He lowered his weapon. "How did he turn?" Noah motioned to Alvin with his head.

"He came back a few days ago. Said he got bit down at the Walmart."

"Did he mention that he left me there to die?"

"Said he was with someone, but he left him 'cause he went crazy. Started threatenin' to kill him."

"Your brother's a liar," he said and then paused, "among other things."

"I know," she squeaked. Brandy lowered her head and hugged her chest. "You gonna kill him?" she asked.

Noah looked back at Alvin who was squirming and snapping. The rope was slowly sliding down toward his stumped wrist.

"No." He moved to the ropes binding Alvin's ankles. "You should get out of here—at least for a little while."

Noah grabbed a rope and began sawing through it with the machete. Once he cut through three quarters of the strand he stopped and then repeated the process on the other rope.

"Why are you doin' that?" she asked.

"Because I want him to get free."

Brandy tilted her head. "Why?"

"I want him to be able to get close to the living, but not touch them. I want him to press his mouth against the meat, but not be able to eat it. Insatiable hunger without a moment's relief. That's the only thing I can do to him now." He stopped sawing and looked out the window. "Maybe that's worse than dying."

Noah turned to leave the room. On his way out, he bent down and pulled Brandy's knife out of the floor.

"Here," he said, handing it to her. "You'll need this."

As Noah walked down the stairs, he plucked the cigarette pack out of his pocket. He pulled a smoke from the box with his mouth and then tucked it back into his shirt. Before stepping outside, he took a knit blanket off the couch and threw it over Dakota's body. She shouldn't have to see him like this, he thought.

He sat on the porch steps and lit the cigarette. A minute later Brandy came out after him. She stood near the door and watched him with curiosity.

Noah exhaled a thick plume of smoke. "I came here because your brother cost me my family." He spoke without looking at her. "And here I've done the same thing to you."

He pulled the rifle off his shoulder and extended it to her.

"You can kill me if you want. I have no one left to come after you."

Brandy looked at the gun, surprised by the gesture. "I don't want to kill you, mister."

Noah looked at her and squinted. "Why not?"

"'Cause I don't want to be left alone."

Noah stared into her big brown eyes seated on two freckled cheeks and finally noticed the resemblance to his sister.

He flicked the cigarette onto the grass and stood up. "My name is Noah," he said holding his hand out to her.

She hesitated and then grasped his hand as if it were an envelope. "Brandy."

Noah smiled. He pulled out the pack of Marlboros from his pocket and set it on the railing.

A loud thump sounded from upstairs.

"Well, Brandy," he said, slinging the rifle over his shoulder, "I think that's our cue to get going."

To be continued….

If you would like to read more stories from the world of *Worse Than Dying*, please email brettvwrites@gmail.com with your email address and book title in the subject line. This address will solely be used to send you an alert when a new story has been published. Please visit www.brettvanvalkenburg.com for more information.

Also, if you enjoyed the book, please consider leaving a review on Amazon.com or whatever website you use to find books. This really helps other readers find stories like WTD, which in turn encourages writers to continue writing. If you *didn't* enjoy the book—uhh—then don't worry about it. No review needed!

Thank you for your patronage and keep reading!

ABOUT THE AUTHOR

Brett Van Valkenburg was born and raised in a small town in upstate New York. At 18 he attended college in central NY and then moved to New York City shortly after graduating. Clearly life has been quite the rollercoaster. Brett currently works for a major financial institution as a Proposal Writer while moonlighting as a fiction and children's book writer. When not penning ramblings about the shambling, Brett spends his time working on a children's book as well as a novel about time travel.

Lightning Source UK Ltd.
Milton Keynes UK
UKHW022108160223
417164UK00024B/268

9 781088 044889